"Help," Zenith shouted.
Would anyone hear her?

Zenith was half-drowned by the time
Steve Forbuck reached her. The water
wasn't deep, but the swirl kept knocking
her over. He carried her back to the
barracks building—found towels, dry
clothes, hot tea.

"I'm sorry," she said. "I didn't believe you
about the flooding."

"What is there about me, Zenith," he
asked dryly, "that makes you like
this—opposite to everything I say or do,
always on the defense?"

She didn't answer him. Suddenly she
knew she might have babbled: Because I
am on the defense, defense for myself. I
don't want to be hurt the way dad may
be hurt, in the way people who love
someone do get hurt ...

She halted her mental babbling sharply.
She didn't love ... she couldn't love ...
why, she disliked this man!

OTHER
Harlequin Romances
by JOYCE DINGWELL

The Boss's Daughter

by

JOYCE DINGWELL

Harlequin Books

TORONTO • LONDON • NEW YORK • AMSTERDAM
SYDNEY • HAMBURG • PARIS

Original hardcover edition published in 1978
by Mills & Boon Limited

ISBN 0-373-02225-5

Harlequin edition published January 1979

CHAPTER ONE

ZENITH coaxed the company jeep up the last short grade of the works hill. At the bend at the top she transferred her foot from the accelerator to the brake, then screeched to a shuddering halt at the town trading post. Climbing inelegantly down, no time for doors, she raced into the store with all the urgency of a fireman rushing to a blaze. (Her father's description.)

'Hi, Bluey,' she called in the rather deep-down voice nature had allotted her, 'where do you hide your Champignons? Not everyday mushrooms, Bluey, *Champignons*, little button ones. Pierre has ordered them, and if that temperamental French cook doesn't get them at once he'll leave in the airstrip bus. That's what he warned, so that's what he'll do. After all' . . . searching a pyramid of cans now . . . 'do you blame him? He's a graduate of the Paris Academy of Cuisine, not a mere Iron Ore Chops and Potatoes man. As well as that he's made it very obvious he doesn't like our Savage Project ways.' Zenith started on another pyramid of cans.

In her absorption she did not see the only other customer in the trading post, but she did hear his voice.

'No wonder he doesn't like them,' the voice said coolly, 'if *your* way is a sample. Stand in a queue like any civilised citizen. The storekeeper is serving me first. He's outside opening up a carton. Wait your turn, son.'

5

Zenith, on a third pyramid, turned herself. She saw, now that her eyes had become accustomed to the cave-dark interior of the post, a tall, thirtyish man in overalls and yellow helmet, meaning precisely nothing, since she wore, and they all wore, protective overalls and safety helmets, too, as it was one of the few things their very tolerant boss, and Zenith's father, really insisted on. Zenith also noted, after a quick informing look at the big, toil-ingrained hands, that the fellow came under Category Manual and not Mechanical. Certainly ... a slight smile ... not Clerical, nor by any stretch of the imagination Executive. Well, she liked that.

'I'm in a hurry,' she said very politely, for she far preferred the Muscle Boys, as she called them, to the White Collar staff, 'so——'

'So nothing,' he came back, unaffected by her sweet approach. 'I was here before you.'

'But this is important.'

'So is my purchase.'

Zenith did not answer that. She had found a can of Champignons (Button) at last. She straightened up from her squat and began to back out of the shop. 'Tell Bluey to book it for me,' she directed, then, realising she had not seen the fellow before so possibly he had not seen her, she added: 'Name of Smith.'

'That's a good one!'

'It's true.'

'Also I'll do no such telling. You wait your turn, you ill-mannered lump.'

She would have stopped to do battle with him, pre-ferred muscle boy though he was, but there was no time. She backed another step and said: 'I have to take this to Pierre at once.'

'Oh, no, you have to stay right here and wait your
turn to be served. I mean that. Good grief, who's your
gang boss? Doesn't he ever jerk you up, tell you
where you get off? Now if you were in my outfit
I'd——'

'*Your* outfit!' Indignation was getting the better of
Zenith. 'And pigs might fly. You don't run any section,
any gang, you can see that by your hands.'

'What's wrong with my hands?' He was holding
them up.

'Nothing, except they belong to a—well——'

'Yes?' he demanded.

'A worker.' She hadn't meant to say that, but he
had asked for it.

'I try to be, boy. I try very hard. And what are you,
then? In some élite category where the word "toil" is a
dirty one, where the syllables that make up "manual
labour" are taboo? Perhaps you're the Company liaison
officer, then? The bio-chemist? Analyst? Supply surveyor? I can tell you you could have fooled me with
those overalls and helmet.'

'We all wear——'

'*Dirty* overalls, *greasy* helmet.'

'They're not!' she snapped.

'Don't answer back.'

Now Zenith was really angry, but for all her rage
another thing came first—the mushrooms for Pierre.
'I'd like to answer back,' she flung, 'and I will later, but
immediately I have other things to do.' Again she
started to retreat.

She did not get far. 'Put that can down,' he called.
'Stay where you are. Wait your turn.'

'I won't!'

'In which case out of the store minus the goods, and when I find out what gang you're attached to, I'll——' The rest of the warning was unintelligible, for the man, recognising rebellion in Zenith's furious face, had stepped forward and lifted her up by the back of her overalls collar. Dangling a foot from the ground, she was too enraged ... also choked ... to heed one word.

But not too enraged to kick. She kicked and she clawed. To do the dangler justice he did neither back to her, but he did bundle her unceremoniously out of the shop. During the bundling, the inevitable happened ... or, thought Zenith wretchedly, she supposed under the circumstances it was inevitable when you were a woman. The man's big hands came in contact with part of her overall top that was *not* firm and muscled and masculine, that was——

He stopped. He swore. He dropped her like a hot cake.

'A female!' he roared.

'Yes!' Zenith gasped, for in the dropping she had lost her footing.

'I wasn't aware that females also worked out here like us poor slobs.'

'No one is poor here,' Zenith defended proudly, 'Savage pay is well above award.'

'I wouldn't know that, I haven't been here long.'

'Obviously,' she said icily.

'My clean gear?' He looked distastefully down on Zenith's own crumple and dust.

'It's a dirty place,' she said, 'iron ore isn't exactly a garden of roses. Also you would know beforehand that there were women here. Even the smallest project runs to a Girl Friday or a secretary.'

'But not a labourer,' he drawled, looking significantly at her, and Zenith flushed.

'I'm not!' She waited a furious moment. 'Helen is our Savage secretary—but you'd be well aware of that in spite of you saying you were unprepared.'

'Helen?' he asked at once.

'Yes.'

'Not a common name,' he observed.

'Nor uncommon,' said Zenith.

'I expect so. How would I be aware of this Helen?'

'Because Helen does all the signing on.'

'Then she hasn't signed me on as yet.'

'She will,' she assured him.

'I see. And who else is there in the gentler sex section?' A sneer to that 'gentler', Zenith noted.

She tilted her chin. 'No doubt you'll discover in due course, even though it will be out of your line.'

'I think you mean a mere labourer's line.'

'Please yourself,' she shrugged.

'Then I'm not pleased.' His eyes were wary.

'At my putting you under Category Manual?'

'No, not that at all, at running into more women. I've had my fill of women ... except——'

'Except?'

'I've just had my fill,' he said again.

'Good, then,' Zenith smiled blandly, 'for apart from several of us, actually only Helen and myself, all the girls are wives, and their husbands wouldn't care much about you hanging around.'

'My fatal charm?'

'I haven't noticed it.'

'You will. But how is it that *you* are hanging around, for I see no ring? Projects are famous for their matri-

monial opportunities. Have you been unsuccessful, or
are you still hoping?'

'I'm here because my father is here,' Zenith said
loftily.

'You mean fathers can bring daughters just as husbands can bring wives? Perhaps uncles their nieces?
Friends can bring their friends? De factos their——'

'No, no, no and no! *I* am different because my father
is different. Name of——'

'Don't tell me, it's Smith. You said so before. But
you can't be Derek Smith's boy, *the* Derek Smith.'

'His girl,' she reminded. 'Yes, I am. I'm the boss's
daughter.'

'Which gives you the right to break queues?'

'No. Yes.' Zenith was not heeding him now, she was
listening instead to an unmistakable sound, the sound
of the departing airstrip bus. 'Pierre——' she said with
an awful certainty, and ran out to the road to see. Her
feeling of awful certainty was right. In the front seat of
the small, converted panel van sat their one-time
French cook, and though Zenith called, waved, danced
up and down, shouted, abused, begged, cajoled, im-
plored and even grovelled, he did not look her way.

'He's gone,' she wept as the bus departed.

'So it seems.' The man had followed her out.

'It's all your fault!' she stormed.

'Then I'm sorry. If you'd said at once——'

'I did.'

'You said Champignons, which, in spite of my being
only Category Manual, I knew were mushrooms.
Surely mushrooms can't be as important as that.'

'They were vitally important. Pierre warned me he
would leave if I didn't return with them in five minutes,
and you—you——'

'No, boss's daughter, *you*. You're not slow to act the grand lady on me, are you, but apparently you can't even control your own domestic staff.'

'One only in the staff. A cook. My father always says an army marches on its stomach, that a good cook is more essential than the highest key man. So he employed Pierre for us.'

'Us?' he queried.

'Dad and me. At least' ... tightly ... 'it was then.'

He ignored the taut note in her voice. 'And now you've gone and lost him,' he mused.

'Yes. Through you. It wouldn't matter so much if *she* wasn't coming, but *she* is, and what am I to do?'

'She?' he queried.

'Coming on the plane that Pierre will leave in.'

'We might be able to catch him,' he suggested.

'No, it's too late, and, anyway, I don't want her to see me like this.'

'I don't wonder at that.' He was looking Zenith up and down, not missing the bad fit of the over-capacious overalls, even longer and wider since the undignified dangling. 'I can see that if *she* did *she* would get the same plane back.' Another of his crooked grins. 'It appears then you really needed this Pierre while *she* was here?'

'Yes.'

'Then you'll have to do the cooking yourself, won't you?'

'I can't,' she sighed. 'I mean, not like that.'

'Not like what?'

'Like first meetings. Like special events. I really mean it's important ... important to Dad.'

'How about the canteen, then?'

'I think it should be more—personal.'

'Then it will have to be you after all, won't it?' He stood pretending concern for her a moment, then he shot back into the trading post and rummaged round for a minute. After a while he returned holding a can opener.

'Here you are, boss's daughter,' he called. 'No need to pay me, I've told Bluey to put it down on your slate. Name of Smith, isn't it?'

'You're a pig!' she snapped angrily.

'Pig iron? It's nothing else but iron up here.'

For a moment Zenith stood struggling for words, then she turned and crossed to the jeep.

'Sorry about the manhandling you got,' he called after her. 'You see, I thought you were.'

'Were?' She looked round at him.

'Male.' He grinned maddeningly.

Wordless again, Zenith climbed into the waggon and started the engine. As she did she heard the works plane zooming in. So Carol had arrived! At once, for they wasted no time, Pierre would have left Savage. What could one do, *what could one*, with a can opener and a can of Champignons?

Zenith sat behind the wheel of the ticking jeep for fully five minutes. She couldn't afford five minutes, but she still sat and tried to think. Out of the corner of her eye she saw the pig depart. He walked with a long pace and in a moment he was out of sight. Actually he should not have been here at all, not at the trading post at this time of the shift, not in his category. Yet what was his category? He had said: 'Now if you were in my outfit I'd——'

What outfit? Also what would he have done?

As it had happened, though, he had done enough,

more than enough. Pierre, always touchy, unenthusi-
astic right from his first day at Savage—an assignment,
he had often sniffed, he only had accepted between
really important callings—had only needed this last
straw to make up his mind.

'There ees no inspiration in thees job,' he had complained bitterly many times, and finally and most bitterly of all only an hour ago, 'no soul, no *joie de vivre*. I
go.'

'Yes, dear Pierre,' Zenith would beg, 'but wait at
least until Carol comes. Carol is important.'

'No one ees important to me when I cannot get the
good ingredients. I am stifled. I am frustrated. I am
bereft.'

'*Oui, cher* Pierre, but until Carol comes. Please!'

'Then till then and then only. I will make the Steak
Superbe, for which I received my special award for the
person.'

'Oh, thank you, Pierre!' she had smiled.

'But only if I get the good ingredients. I will require
steak.'

'Done.' There were ample steaks in the deep freeze.

'Then Champignons.'

'They're mushrooms,' Zenith had nodded. 'I'm
afraid they'll have to be canned.'

'Regrettably,' Pierre had agreed, 'I will accept that.
But they must be button-small, and if you do not bring
them in time to undergo the special marinade that em-
braces the steak, then I leave, mademoiselle.'

'I love you, Pierre, and so does Papa, and so, I'm
sure, will Carol,' Zenith had assured him.

But Carol would never love him, for she would
never see him, or if she did as she passed him on the

strip she would not know. The necessary Champignons, because of that pig-iron man, were late, and Pierre had given Zenith no second chance. Probably he had been waiting for something like this, had been waiting ever since he had come here. He had never liked it. He had gone off with his elegant French grip that Zenith suspected he had never unpacked, and she was left with a can opener, a can and a father who relied upon her to make a good first show.

What to do? *What?*

As usual, as she had done from the first day she had met Dad's secretary, Zenith went in search of Helen.

Beyond the trading post was a cluster of buildings. The cluster housed the white collar side of Savage Mining. There were offices marked in the names that that pig-iron man had thrown at her ... Liaison Officer, Bio-Chemist, Analyst, Supply Surveyor. There was also Accountant, and as she tried to scurry past *that* door, Brent Davids came to the portal.

Zenith did not want to see Brent. Apart from her not having the time, he was never her favourite male. That was unfair to him, she knew, especially when he always wanted to see her, but, in the way of projects isolated from civilisation, failing any other eligible male to supply friendly gossip, she had been coupled with Brent, and she disliked it.

She called quickly : 'Hi, Brent. I'm in a hurry.' She scurried to the next office marked : 'Secretary'. She knocked, then opened and entered, after which she wailed : 'Oh, Helen !'

Derek Smith's secretary Helen sat at her desk, and she took off her glasses and looked across and smiled at Zenith.

'I think I've heard that cry of distress before,' she soothed. 'Trouble?'

'Dire,' sighed Zenith. 'Pierre has finally gone. Really gone this time.'

'Oh, you poor dear!'

That was the lovely part of Helen, she always sympathised. She could have reminded: 'Well, you knew it was coming,' but being Helen she only wanted to help.

She was a lovely woman, or at least Zenith saw her like that. She was middle-aged, easily old enough to be Zenith's mother, and she had a smile that reached her eyes, those gentle eyes that now were being kind again behind the glasses which she had put back. For the rest she had thick hazel hair with a few shining threads of silver in it and a quiet air of listening. I'd have liked her for my mother, Zenith had often thought.

'What am I to do, Helen?' she asked. 'Dad's already gone out to fetch her.'

'Who, Carol?'

'Yes.'

'Then no panic, Zenith, Derek said he'd give Miss Quinn a Cook's Tour of the works before he brought her back. That should take a while.'

'What can we do in a while?' groaned Zenith.

In typical Helen spirit Helen responded at once:

'A lot.'

'Like?'

'What do you want?'

'Steak Superbe?' tried Zenith.

'Perhaps not that, I wouldn't know how, anyway, but we can get something from the canteen and pretty it up.'

'You mean——'

'Yes, I mean just that. What have you in stock in the way of embellishment, Zenith? Some pimento? olives? capers? capsicum? That sort of thing?'

'Yes, but——'

'A nice cloth ready? Candles?'

'Yes.'

'Then you're saved,' Helen announced.

'Am I? I have as much idea of dressing up a meal as I have of dressing up myself, after this year at Savage.'

'That's another thing—you must look nice. You at least must look like a girl.'

'Not a lump?'

'A lump? You were never anything like that.'

'No?' About to tell Helen she had been called one only a few minutes ago, Zenith changed her mind. There were other things, urgent things, to discuss.

'You're serious, Helen? You will help?'

'Your father definitely won't be let down, I promise you,' smiled Helen. 'Now you go back to the house and start dressing ... dress both yourself and the table ... and I'll see Jake.' Jake ran the canteen for Savage. 'Then,' continued Helen, 'I'll bring round the spoils and we'll get to work together.'

'Helen, you're wonderful!' smiled Zenith in relief.

'It's nothing,' Helen refused. 'Nothing when it's for —for the boss.'

'... And the future Mrs Boss?' Zenith said in unmistakable distaste.

Helen did not answer that, all at once she seemed to have found something to be attended to on her desk.

'Oh, Helen, why?' Zenith could not help herself. 'Why? Why? *Why?*'

Sharp for Helen who was never sharp, the older woman reprimanded: 'Enough of that!'

'Enough of what?'

'You know very well, Zenith.'

'But——' Zenith began.

'I'll see Jake, get something, then bring it down. I'll also' ... a look at Zenith ... 'bring down Brent Davids, or give him a reminder.'

'Oh, Helen!' Zenith sighed ruefully.

'Sorry, Zenith, but that's what your father wants. He also' ... a little hunch of her nicely rounded shoulders ... 'asked for me.'

'Of course.'

'Plus a sixth, a male, to make the numbers up. I wasn't told the name, but obviously the invited one knows all about it.'

'Dad did this?'

'Yes, dear. Perhaps three for dinner, a first dinner, didn't seem quite right, so——'

'He could have told me he wanted it tête-à-tête and I would have eaten in the canteen,' said Zenith crossly.

'Don't be so touchy, dear. Try to put yourself in your father's place.'

'Bringing a bride-to-be years younger than himself to the camp, you mean?'

'Zenith!'

'Oh, I'm sorry. Believe me, I am very sorry, Helen. I've nothing against this Carol, and particularly her age, which Father has told me several anxious times is only a few years more than my age, it's just——'

'Yes, Zenith?'

'Oh, I don't know. It's just that I never knew my mother. She died too early. But if I had a mother ... if

I had . if I had one now ... Helen, what are you doing?'

'Pushing you out. Perhaps if you'd moved yourself in the first place we wouldn't be in this position. Your father is bringing in his fiancée, Zenith, and not all the talk in the world can alter that. We have to get ready a dinner for six—Mr Smith, Mr Smith's fiancée, Mr Smith's daughter, Mr Smith's accountant, secretary, and a sixth, Mr Smith's something or other, to make up the number.'

'But, Helen——

'The plane is in. She—Miss Carol Quinn—has arrived. Your father is showing her the open cuts. He's describing what happens after the ore is won. He's introducing her to the works managers, the gang bosses, and, because he's Derek Smith, the labourers.'

... And including somewhere a tall, loose-limbed character who dangled me by my overalls collar, Zenith thought, who called me a lump, who dropped me at once when he found out I was a——

'Yet we still stand wasting time,' Helen continued. 'Get cracking, Zenith. And let me get cracking, too.'

Not giving Zenith an opportunity to argue, Helen pushed past her and went out of the office in the direction of the canteen.

More deliberately Zenith followed her ... and yes, Brent was still at his door.

'I'll be seeing you later,' he called. So he had not forgotten.

'Yes, Brent,' Zenith replied.

She walked across to the jeep.

Carol, her father, Helen, Brent, herself ... who else? There were few bachelors at Savage, and it would have to be a bachelor, for a married man would have brought his wife along, too, and that would have made not six but seven. So who else?

Zenith got into the waggon and released the brake.

CHAPTER TWO

How would Dad's Carol react to this scenery? Zenith mulled this over as she descended in the jeep to the boss's house. It was not pretty terrain she travelled, in fact it was quite the reverse, but there was something about it that grabbed at you, that often never let you go. Not only Zenith had found that out, nearly all the Savages, as they called themselves, had as well. Once the ochre country enfolded you, you were forever enslaved.

It was bareboned land. Even embellished as it was now by the vegetation that had spread following the Big Wet and the breaking up of the Lucy River, you were aware of those hard bones. It was fierce country, savage as its name of Savage, and yet at times it could be almost hurtingly tender, for iron ore places possessed that witchery. The softening purplish aura that cloaked everything in a red-mauve veil achieved this unexpected gentleness, and it was the direct result of ore. Ore even seemed to stain the air. For the rest it was pumice-dry, rough-hewn, treeless except for a few stands of tattered gums, yet still achieving a magnificence that it did not really possess by its wide, inverted bowl of heraldic, quite stunning blue sky.

Zenith had loved it from the day she had first set

foot on it, and that was seven years ago when her
father had brought her here for her school vacation.
After the ample but naturally fenced fields of Retford
Girls' School, it had seemed limitless.

'I feel like one of the Ungirt Runners,' young Zenith
had rejoiced. 'We did that poem this year.'

Her father had been pleased with her enthusiasm,
but still he had warned: 'No matinees here, Zennie, no
regatta teas, no anything really.'

'I still love it, Dad.' Young Zenith had looked
shrewdly up at him. 'Just like you do.'

'So it shows, does it? Yes, it's my country. And as
though to repay my love it's giving itself to me. Giving
lavishly. Zenith, you're going to be Miss Moneybags
very soon.'

'Thank you, Mr Moneybags. I gather then that we're
rich.'

'We will be in a few years. Oh, I won't be one of the
big fish, but quite big enough. It was a lucky day I came
out fossicking to Savage and recognised what I did.'

'Not luck, Dad,' she pointed out, 'you tried long
enough.'

'Lots of men try, Zen, but I got the jackpot.'

'Can I leave school and come and look after you?' she
asked.

'I'm well looked after by the canteen, and you will
finish school,' was her father's answer.

'But after that?'

'If you're still of the same mind.'

'Of course I will be, Dad.'

'Yes, I believe that. But one thing concerns me.'

'What, Dad?' she had asked.

'Eligible men. I'm supposing you'll marry one day.'

'I suppose so.' Zenith had given a careless shrug.

Derek Smith had frowned. 'There won't be much husband material here, Zenith. I intend trying to attract the married men mostly, by providing comfortable family houses and charging a minimum rent. In that way one is assured of at least four or five years' service, something very valuable in our Top End. Mostly the bachelors only accumulate a big bank balance, and then hit south.'

'Can we meet that when it comes, Dad?'

'Of course, girl.'

'And can I come up every break?'

'Every break.'

'Then finally at seventeen can I——'

'Eighteen,' he corrected.

'Oh, Dad!'

'*Eighteen.*'

'Then at eighteen,' Zenith had resigned herself, 'I'll be here for good.'

'I think it will have to be for good, Puss, there's nowhere to get into mischief at Savage.'

Zenith had laughed, she remembered, and wished her years away, and presto, they *had* melted, and at eighteen, a year ago now, she had come to Savage. For good.

She had reached the boss's house by now, and she drew up.

The building was no bigger and no better than any of the other project family quarters, and that went for the interior as well. Zenith gnawed at her lip. She wondered how Miss Carol Quinn would like that.

It was a pre-fab, they all were, and in its transport here over unmade roads had met with the expected mishaps. In short it was distinctly tatty and shabby. The furniture in particular had fared badly. What had not lost a leg or suffered a broken mirror had been chipped and scratched.

However, she had done her best with bright curtains, and yesterday she had gone bush and carted back a jeep-full of goodies, red desert pea, flood iris from a left-over pond that had appeared following the last rains, most of all the fiercely blue Salvatian Jane. She had arranged them everywhere, and she had been pleased with the result. Her father had stopped short when he had seen them, then he had turned and smiled: 'You have your mother's gift.'

'Was she good at it, Dad?'

'She could make a Chelsea Flower Show out of a fistful of dandelions.'

'Poor Dad,' sighed Zenith, 'I should have dressed up the house before.'

'You've been as busy as I have, Puss, there wasn't time. But I'm glad you've done it now.'

'For—Carol?'

'Yes, Zen, it will be a kind of welcome, won't it?'

Zenith had nodded—but she had stopped rearranging the position of a Jane, stopped uncrumpling a flood iris. Welcome to Carol, she had thought hollowly, welcome to Carol, not to—— She had turned away.

Fortunately her father had left the room by now, she would not have hurt him for the world, but—Carol. Why, oh, why Carol? Why not——

She had tried to remind herself of the tenderness she had felt for Dad on that night he had told her his news. He had just returned from a trip to Sydney ... and there had been something different about him.

'Zenith,' he had said.

'Yes, Father? Please note that I'm saying Father, Dad, because somehow you look very handsome to-night. Quite fascinating, in fact.'

'With my grey thatch! But I'm glad about the good-looking bit.'

'I said handsome,' she reminded him.

'I'm glad because ... well, to put it briefly, Zen, something happened this time.'

'In Sydney?'

'Yes.' A pause. 'Zen, it's been a long time since Elvie died.'

'Nineteen years,' Zenith had nodded.

'It wasn't duty to you that kept me unmarried, and it wasn't undying love, as the novels say, for Elvie would have hated that, it was—well, I just never met anyone, Zen.'

... Helen? Helen, Dad? Zenith had longed to burst it out, but she had not.

'Yes, Father?' she had prompted instead.

'Now I *have* met someone, Zenith. I—I feel for her very much, and she feels for me in return.'

'Then that's just wonderful, darling.' Zenith had managed to imbue enthusiasm into her voice, but it had not been easy.

'You mean you don't mind?'

'Mind your happiness? Oh, Dad!'

'I assure you that you'll never be deprived, Zennie, I mean there's more than enough for——'

'For six wives?' Now why had she said that? It wasn't funny.

At once she had amended: 'You mean I'll just be Miss Slightly Lighter Moneybags?' She had laughed.

'Tell me about her, Dad. Name of——?'

'Carol. Carol Quinn.' A pause. 'Zenith, she's beautiful. An old dodger like I am and that beautiful girl——'

'Girl?' she queried.

'Well, this is the difficult part. You see, she's ... well ... well, she's not much older than you, Zen.' An anxious look. 'Are you shocked?'

'Shocked? Of course not. How silly!'

But Zenith *had* been shocked. Not shocked because of the years between her father and this Carol, but shocked because of Helen. Helen was nearly the same age as Dad, the same age her mother would have been. That had been the shock. And the hurt.

'How silly,' she had scorned again, and he had believed her.

'I would never have dared approach her, but—well, she approached me,' Derek had laughed delightedly.

... Did she know who you were, Zenith had wondered privately, had someone named you Mr Moneybags?

'Zennie, she *cares* for me. She explained how some girls need maturity, must have it.'

... I bet she did! Again Zenith had said it to herself.

'And—and that's all there is to it really. Just May and December ... *and love*. I suppose I'm an old fool, but I feel like I haven't felt for years.'

'Then, Dad, that's enough.' Zenith had taken a deep breath and said it firmly. It was enough, it must be, Dad's happiness was all that mattered, everything else was unimportant.

They had smiled across at each other, then Zenith

had been told that Carol was coming up to Savage. Derek had rather diffidently suggested to his daughter that she spread the news around, get the project accustomed to it.

'For Carol believes we shouldn't wait too long,' he had said, 'and even though I'm urging her to be quite sure, I believe our Savages should be told.'

'I'd better think of moving to single quarters, Dad.'

'Not yet. You see, Carol spoke of alternating our time later between here and Sydney, in which case——'

Between Savage and Sydney. *Sydney*. Dad would die in Sydney, he was intrinsically a hard-core, red country man. But Zenith had kept silent.

'Very well,' she had agreed.

'You'll tell the project people, then? I—well, I feel rather embarrassed telling them myself.'

'There should be no embarrassment in true love, Dad, but I know what you mean.'

'Thank you, Zen. Oh, and particularly mention it to —Helen, won't you?'

'Dad——' Zenith began.

'Odd,' he confessed, 'but I feel quite reluctant to tell Helen. We've been working together too long, I expect. We've become—brother and sister.'

'Helen doesn't look like your sister to me.'

'All the same, Zenith, will you tell her?'

Zenith had told Helen, and all she could have reported afterwards was that Helen had taken off her glasses, polished them, then put them back again.

'I hope Mr Smith will be very happy,' she had said flatly.

'Helen——'

'He's a fine man—indeed, the finest. I'm sure we all wish him joy.'

'Helen——' began Zenith again.

'Most of all his daughter would wish it, wouldn't she?'

'Helen.' This time Zenith had managed to break through. 'Helen, why? Why?'

Helen had answered the same as she had answered a few moments ago. 'Enough of that.' They had not discussed it since.

They were not going to discuss it now—Helen had made that very clear back in her office. How could they? It was beyond question, it was a final conclusion, a *fait accompli* ... or almost so. If Zenith had had any doubts about that, then Helen was bringing some containers from the canteen to be dressed up, and she, Zenith, was to dress up the table to match, dress up herself.

She would start with the latter, she decided. She walked down the hall to the bathroom, taking an almost mean pleasure in the deliberately bare floor ... it was too warm for carpets up here ... and the very plain, rather ugly, functional furniture. How would Miss Quinn like the decor?

She threw off her clothes and turned on the taps full strength, hard stinging strength, to take her mind off— well, Carol. To take her mind off that pig, too, for she was angrily reminded of him by the beginnings of a bruise at the top of her breast. Manhandled had been an apt word. She glowered at the faintly purple spot.

She got out of the shower and chose a rough towel. By the time she had finished she had rubbed away both Carol and him. She dressed, protected herself

with a pinafore, then came out again. Through one of
the windows she saw Helen pull up in her small car,
saw her carrying in a large pot of something covered
with a napkin. She saw her going back for more
material.

So the dinner for six was on the move.

'What is it, Helen?' Zenith looked at the container
curiously.

'Humble stew at present, but at dinner tonight a
very palatable beef Stroganoff ... I hope. Get out the
embellishments and we'll start the magic. I thought
some golden rice would add a touch.'

Zenith took out everything she could find and began
setting the table. A lace cloth and candles made it
festive at once.

'Your decorations are lovely, dear.' Helen paused in
her labours.

'Thank you, Helen, but I wonder if they'll make up
for a dozen long-stemmed roses. Red' ... an edge to
Zenith's voice ... 'for true love.'

'I'm sure they will. Zenith——'

'Yes, Helen?'

'Can't you start thinking about your father instead?'

'Instead of what?'

'I was going to say instead of yourself.'

'But I'm not ... well, I suppose I am in a way. You
see, I don't want—I don't want——'

'Can't you start thinking about your father, Zenith?'
interrupted Helen sharply.

'Are *you* thinking about him, are you being the
perfect secretary as usual? The faultless automaton?'
Zenith bit her lip in annoyance. 'Oh, Helen, I'm sorry!'

'Forgiven. Also I'm thinking about him, and that's why I'm presenting the best Stroganoff I can.'

'What if I open my big mouth at the crucial moment and say "This is really project stew and not what you think"?'

'Then you'll be duly dealt with, and I believe I know just the person.' Helen forgot her concentration a moment to chuckle to herself.

Zenith thought she knew one, too, and she writhed, but she did not let Helen see.

'Did you find out about the sixth guest?' she asked instead.

'Yes.' Again Helen smiled privately.

'One of the married men whose wife is down south at present?' supposed Zenith.

'No, a legitimate bachelor. Incidentally, I wish he and Brent Davids would come. I'd like them here before the guests of honour arrive.'

'Well, they won't be, that looks like Dad's car now.' Up here you could tell when a car was coming long before you could see the car, there was always a warning distant blob of red dust.

Helen said : 'Bother,' and kept on embellishing.

The dust blob grew bigger. The car took shape. Then at the same moment as the car drew up at the bottom of the steps two men came in by the side entrance.

'Perfect timing,' applauded Helen. 'Now I won't have to unroll a red carpet.'

'Red carpet?' queried a voice that Zenith felt she had heard before.

'We haven't any,' she informed the voice, trying to remember, at the same time nodding to Brent, then turning to nod to the other man, the one who had just spoken, but finding his back turned on her.

Brent Davids was turning now, too, turning to the door. Helen and Zenith duly turned.

Derek Smith and his fiancée were climbing the shallow steps to the verandah, they were walking down the hall. The girl had her hand lightly on Dad's shoulder, and he walked very tall, proudly aware of her pretty gesture of dependence.

But—pretty? Oh, no, that was a very wrong word. She was never just pretty, she was beautiful. Just absolutely, beyond any argument lovely, her colouring, her features, her bearing, her poise ... oh, the lot.

Zenith heard the stifled intake of breath from Helen, saw Brent straighten himself up, saw——

She saw the man who had come to make up a sixth step back the slightest inch from the approaching couple ... or rather from the approaching girl. As though ... well, as though he had known her before. But wouldn't anyone who had previously met a girl like that step *forward*, not back?

Then, in his step back, she saw the man's profile, hard, controlled, a faintly dominant chin.

Why, it was him. The pig. Pig-Iron, as she had been calling him to herself. The manhandler.

'This is quite a welcome,' Dad was saying. 'Carol, my dear, meet my daughter, my secretary, my accountant and my new right hand, determined to go through as I went through, not only using that right hand but both hands.

'Carol Quinn,' he went on more intimately, 'soon to be Carol Smith, meet Zenith, Helen, Brent, Steve.'

He extended his arms to them all.

Helen had drinks ready and they made the usual toasts. After this Zenith took Carol to her room.

It looked quite attractive, Zenith thought. Suffering a guilty conscience because of her real feelings she had made an extra effort with every detail.

She need not have bothered. Carol obviously noticed nothing. She threw down her handbag and scarf on the bed, then sat beside them.

'Oh, lord!' she sighed.

'Was it a tiring trip?' asked Zenith.

'No, but it was—oh, never mind. Let's go out and get the thing over.'

'I thought you might care to wash.'

' "Down the hall", no doubt.'

'Well, yes, you see these are prefabs and——'

'Spare me the dreary rest. I'll find it.' The girl had got up again and she reached the door before Zenith could reach it to show her to the bathroom. But once there, she paused.

'How long have you had Steve Forbuck here?' she demanded.

'Forbuck?' queried Zenith.

'That fellow outside. The taller one.'

'I would say only a short time before you.'

'Interesting,' drawled Carol.

'I don't know ... I really mean I don't know him.'

'But you know the other, Brent Something?'

'Brent Davids?'

'Yes.'

'Then yes, I do know him.'

'I see. Rather nice for him.' A short laugh.

A little uncertainly, for Zenith did not know whether to take that as nice for Brent because she,

Zenith, was nice, or as nice for him because of her advantageous position as the boss's daughter, Zenith began hurriedly reciting the speech she had prepared.

'I hope you'll be very happy here—we all hope so. Of course in the beginning it may seem a little strange, after all it is a strange part of Australia, but——'

'Keep it for later.' Carol stepped away from Zenith and went and ran water over her slim white hands, one of them flashing a diamond ring. Then she returned to the front room, accepted another drink.

Helen caught Zenith's eye, and the two of them went out to the kitchen and served up the project stew that had changed now into a beef Stroganoff. They did it silently. Not a word between them.

But silence made no difference to the dish. Derek Smith proclaimed it quite superb, the best ever.

'We have a French chef,' he told Carol proudly.

'*Had*——' began Zenith, but was stopped by someone kicking her under the table. It was not Helen, for Helen had gone out to the kitchen for something or other.

'But unfortunately, dear,' Dad was continuing, 'Pierre only creates, never serves.'

It would not be Brent, he would not be aware that Pierre had departed. Leaving——Zenith gave the sixth guest the slightest glance and received the slightest nod in reply.

It was a fairly successful meal. Carol did not eat very much, but she drank in every word. Her violet-grey eyes, larger and more luminous than eyes should be, rested on each speaker as he spoke, for it was always 'he', neither Zenith nor Helen offered anything to the conversation, nor did Carol seek them out.

Fortunately there was no need to attend to the used dishes. They might not have a cook, but they had, and always had had, a dishwasher.

Helen and Zenith stacked and packed, switched on, and came back to the lounge.

Perhaps tonight it might have been better if they had needed to do things manually, at least it would have broken up the evening. But they had mechanical help, and could not, without appearing foolish, turn their backs on it. Instinctively they both looked at the clock and saw that it only stood at eight.

Zenith noticed Carol looking restlessly around.

Now was the time surely for that tête-à-tête between Dad and his fiancée. She looked across at Brent, willing him to get up.

Brent did get up, but it was with a proposal.

'The night is young. How about going over to the canteen and watching the weekly hop?'

'I'm sure Carol——' Zenith tried.

'Yes, I feel you'll be tired, dear,' Derek Smith came in.

'Not tired at all. Quite anxious to see more. Will I do like this, or do we dress up?'

There was nothing more to be said. They all walked out of the house and up the short hill and into the recreation room. Here an orchestra from the works assembled each Friday and tried out their latest numbers.

A deep gloom had settled on Zenith. This was not right, she thought. It was not, anyway, as her father would naturally want it.

But Derek Smith was sitting and smiling, encouraging Brent, if he needed any encouragement, to ask Carol to dance. It was a very mod number, and Dad wouldn't have had a clue, Zenith knew.

Steve Forbuck got Helen up. Helen protested, but made a heroic attempt, and her father was full of admiration.

'Our Helen will try anything, she's a great old man.'

'She's not an old man, Dad,' protested Zenith.

'It's just a phrase. Now I ...'

'If it was your period you'd beat them all.' Zenith said the last to herself; she had had an idea. She went to Jim, the bandleader, and had a word in his ear.

'Sure,' he grinned, 'anything for the boss. How about *The Blue Danube*?'

'Not that far back. Some nice, medium period waltz.'

'Done!'

At once the brisk music was changing its beat.

Partners were changing, too. Zenith was pleased to see her father, encouraged by familiar music, getting up and making his way towards his fiancée.

But something happened before Dad got there. Brent stepped across and claimed Zenith, and when she turned again, Steve Forbuck was dancing with Carol. That left Helen for Dad, which should have pleased Zenith, and would have, except that Carol and Steve slid by them at that moment, and they slid so tightly they could have been one dancer only, one pair of arms, one pair of legs, a single breath.

'Well now,' commented Brent, deciding to try to emulate them.

Zenith drew back and just at that moment there was another musical break.

This time Dad did get Carol. Brent got Helen.

Unenthusiastically but inevitably Zenith turned into the arms of Steve Forbuck.

They began moving round the floor.

CHAPTER THREE

AT once it was obvious that this was not to be a two-figures-merged-into-one affair. Steve Forbuck held Zenith erectly ... and a full foot away. It reminded Zenith of period movies with the ladies and gentlemen moving around in stately, elegant and oh-so-uncompromising measure. She wriggled her hand away from his a moment to kill a near-hysterical giggle.

'Not quite cheek to cheek, is it?' he said, reading the gesture. 'Would you like me to correct that?'

'No, certainly not!' Just to make sure Zenith caught the bandleader's eye, and he grinned and broke off the waltz and started some pop.

At once Dad and Carol left the floor, followed closely by Brent and Helen. Zenith went to leave as well, but Steve Forbuck replaced the hand that had dropped away when the music had changed and began gyrating her round instead, apparently loosely, but actually even more tightly than his and Carol's close grasp had been.

'I don't want to dance this,' Zenith protested.

'But you asked for it. Oh, yes, you did, I saw you nod. And what you ask for, you certainly get, don't you? You must have realised that earlier today.'

Angrily Zenith said: 'I've realised quite a lot of things today.'

'You intrigue me, boss's daughter.' He whirled her

round again; he certainly knew the new generation dancing, Zenith thought.

But in spite of everything Zenith found herself enjoying the change of rhythm. As the only contemporary single partner for the Savage bachelors she was aware that she had got to the stage of doing this kind of thing really well. So she did it now ... and was a little piqued when Steve not only kept up with her but kept her busy keeping up with him.

'You've been around,' she panted at last.

'A string of projects before this and the weekly hop the sole social diversion,' he shrugged in explanation.

'A string of projects! Wouldn't they keep you on, then?'

'I left on my own accord. They didn't have what I was looking for.'

'Has Savage?' she asked.

'I don't know, but I think ... I have a feeling ...' He glanced away, and Zenith followed the direction of the look. His eyes were on the table where the boss and his guests sat. Also the boss's fiancée.

'In case you misunderstand, my father and Miss Quinn are engaged to be married,' Zenith said stiffly.

'I didn't misunderstand,' he assured her.

'Then——?'

'But I think *you* are trying to misunderstand when you act so self-righteously. In your heart you no more want Miss Quinn to marry your father than you want' —he paused, then grinned—'than you want me for your husband.'

'You're right about that, you'd be the last one I would want, but still wrong about Dad. I want the world for Dad.'

'But not a world marked Carol? Oh, yes, it was very obvious right from the beginning, for all your pains not to show it. What is it? You don't like the idea of one day sharing the loot with a *Mrs* Moneybags, Miss Moneybags?'

'You're intolerable!' she said angrily.

'But right?'

Furiously she turned the tables on him. 'You said I was obvious, but what about you yourself?'

'I? Obvious?'

'You'd met Carol Quinn before—I saw that at once.'

'How did you see it?'

'You—well, you were aroused.' It was the only word Zenith could think of at the moment.

'Wouldn't that girl arouse anyone? You should have seen your boy-friend's face.'

'Brent's?'

'Who else?'

'He is not,' she contradicted.

'Not?'

'Not my boy-friend.'

'Perhaps not tonight, nor tomorrow, nor even next week. But eventually?'

'No.'

'I can't accept that. You see, I also saw his face when he first looked at you. Prior to looking at Carol, of course.'

'Of course,' Zenith said acidly.

'Davids was blinded by you,' he went on.

'As you are blinded by her?'

'As I am not, and never was. Never will be.'

'Well, *I* can't accept that. However, one thing has been established: you *have* met Miss Quinn before. I even believe she's the reason you left wherever you came from. She didn't react to that "fatal charm" of yours, so you took off. There's nothing' ... warming to her subject ... 'like a man spurned.'

'Nor a female's imagination. Incidentally, the correct quotation is "Nor hell a *fury*", and the subject is a *woman*. Have you had enough?'

'Of what?'

'This dance. Because I have. Also I've had enough of you.' He waited, then when she did not respond, he asked : 'May I return you to the fold?' Without waiting he did so.

Soon afterwards the party left the dance.

Zenith went to bed the moment she reached home. At last, she thought, Dad and Carol will be able to talk in private. But if there was any talk, it was very brief. Hardly had she closed the door than she heard Carol's door close. The girl could be tired, she supposed, but—— Inexplicably uneasy, Zenith put out her light.

Carol's door was still shut when Zenith came out the next morning.

Dad was gone; he had never been a white collar boss. No doubt he was down one of the open cuts now, moving from outfit to outfit like he always did, getting as dirty as the workers as he did so, not caring one jot. How would Carol like that?

Zenith made tea and went tentatively to the girl's door. When she did not answer her quiet knock, she turned the handle and looked in. Carol was asleep, her pale hair all over the pillow, her white arms outflung, as lovely without make-up as she was with it. It was quite unfair. Zenith put down the tea and withdrew again. It was time she opened up her nursery school.

She was not a proper teacher, but she had done voluntary kindergarten work in Sydney during her final college year, and when her father had suggested it, and when the mothers had welcomed it, she had become very keen on the little pre-school. Dad had recommended it in case she found time heavy on her hands after the first exploratory months, and the mothers had liked it, for it gave them the feeling that their little ones were not being deprived of what city toddlers were provided with.

A pre-fab had been set aside and furnished in the usual way, from rocking horses and monkey puzzles to miniature railways, blackboards and the time-honoured brown teddy bear.

Zenith found an envelope and wrote : 'Look around, Carol, do anything you like. I'll be in the nursery school and eager to offer you a sleeping mat.' She hoped Carol would be able to smile over that last. One couldn't tell at once how people felt about children.

She found her smock, a loose pink one with immense pockets, since with children you always needed king-sized pockets, and left the house.

As she walked to her small pupils, Zenith felt her cares leaving her.

The matchbox pre-fab buildings ... really strong buildings, but they always appeared matchbox erections to Zenith ... seemed as natural as a tree-lined avenue to a suburban housewife. The perpetual noise, sometimes stridently harsh and penetrating, sometimes only a soft throb, was as acceptable as birdsong.

There was a changeover whistle shrilling now; in Savage a shift seemed always to be changing, and

Zenith smiled at the long, resounding sibilation. One gang off at the open cut, one gang on.—His gang? Forbuck's? Who was he? Who was this Steve Forbuck Dad had taken on? Why had he come? He had had a string of project jobs before this one; Dad should have looked into that. So many previous jobs didn't sound good.

Zenith turned into her pre-school.

Half a dozen mothers anxiously awaited her. They would hand over their toddlers whom actually out here they had all the time in the world and more to superintend, then proceed to pottery or basket weaving classes which the majority of them weren't very interested in, anyway. However, it gave them the same indulged feeling that their city sisters could have, and that made for a more contented wife, and a contented wife made for a husband who would stay on at Savage, and that's what all this was about.—But what about Carol? Zenith frowned. She had no children to deposit here, at Dad's age probably wouldn't; also Carol looked the last in the world to sink herself into basket weaving or the rest. Or babies, should it happen after all. However ... and Zenith set her teeth ... Dad had said that part of their married time would be spent in Sydney. Where will that put me? she wondered.

She accepted small Marcella from Joan Lintott, Peter from Mary Burton.

'Zenif,' said Marcella importantly, 'you know the barf?'

Oh, yes, Zenith knew the barf. The bath had been a necessary inclusion in the pre-school equipment. Out here in summer the temperature could climb steeply and very uncomfortably, and a bath was a necessary adjunct to a kindergarten, for in a climate like this children quickly dehydrated and had to be regularly dunked and cooled off. There was going to be a pool built one day, but until then——

'Yes, Marcella,' Zenith said, 'I know the bath.'

'Then you know Alexander?'

'Yes, I know Alexander.'

'Then Alexander is putting things in it.'

'In the bath?'

'Yes.'

'Well, dear, if it's empty . . .'

'It's not,' announced Marcella. 'He fulled it.'

Alexander was one of Zenith's three-year-olds, small, square, independent . . . and a broth of a boy.

'At first,' went on Marcella with enjoyment, 'it was the rubber ducks. Then' . . . a pause for a good effect . . . 'more.'

'More?' queried Zenith.

'More.'

'Oh,' said Zenith, beginning to hurry.

Alexander, hearing her approach, acted quickly. He threw all their chalk, a stool, a doll's house, Hugo their big brown bear and finally himself, clothed and sandalled, in.

'All hot,' he explained to Zenith.

Zenith bailed out, including Alexander in the bail-out, dried Hugo, then started the day with Thank You, God.

'Does God have barfs?' asked Alexander. 'Is God clean or dirty?'

'Clean,' assured Zenith. She did not reply to the bath question in case it encouraged Alexander to dunk himself again in religious fervour. Instead she veered him to a new interest, and the morning meandered on.

When she had written her note earlier, Zenith had not expected Carol to respond. She was pleased, and a little ashamed of herself for thinking ungraciously, when around eleven the girl strolled in.

'There *is* a school!' Carol looked incredulous. 'I thought you were joking.'

'Even that sleeping mat I offered you is genuine,' grinned Zenith. 'There is a more advanced place of learning, of course, but it still only deals with the primaries. After primary school the kids either have to go south to college or to government hostels.'

Carol patently was not interested.

'Poor you, and I imagined you queening it up here.'

'You're sorry for me because I'm doing this?'

'Yes.'

'But I do it because I want to,' Zenith assured her.

'Let me get this straight: it's voluntary?'

'Yes.'

'No pay?'

'No. Dad suggested it in the first place, he was afraid I would get bored with nothing to do.'

'You could say that again,' Carol said feelingly.

Zenith looked covertly at her. The girl couldn't be bored this early, surely. But looking at Carol availed you nothing ... except the unarguable fact once more that she was exceptionally beautiful. Zenith had thought so last night with candlelight, but now she *knew* so in the bright, searching, revealing light of the north Australian inland.

'Looked enough?' insinuated Carol at last.

'Oh ... I'm sorry.'

'Forgiven,' Carol shrugged.

'I was really looking to see if you were sick of Savage already,' Zenith dared.

'So far I've been far from sick of it,' Carol smiled blandly.

'But—later?'

'We won't be here later.'

'Oh, yes, Dad did tell me how you planned a city house in between.'

'Just stop at city house,' Carol advised, 'for that's how it will be in the end.'

'But Dad——' began Zenith.

'Anything else besides that mat to show me?' Carol broke in. 'No? Then I'll go and renew my acquaintance with Brent. I noticed his office on my way here.' She stopped at the nursery door, then turned and looked at Zenith. 'No objection?' she smiled.

'Objection?'

'At my visiting Brent.'

'If you're supposing by that that he and I have something between us, we have not,' Zenith said bluntly.

'No, I didn't suppose that. Though I could have, couldn't I? After all, he was there last night.'

'So were others. There was Helen——'

'Oh, yes, Helen.' A slight smile.

'There was also—Mr Forbuck.'

'Steve.' Now a full smile played round Carol's full red mouth. However, she did not say any more about the new man, she returned to Brent.

'I hope I haven't upset anything there, Zenith. Davids, I mean.'

'How could you, when there is nothing to upset?' shrugged Zenith.

'Not on your part, or so you say, but—his?'

'If you're meaning did I notice how instantly attracted he was to you, Carol, then the answer is Yes.'

'How honest you are! I'll be honest back, then. Any interest from him would be of little interest to me, and do be assured of that. I'm too accustomed to such things.' A little pat to Carol's perfect hair.

'Also,' Carol went on, 'if it cheers you at all it was not my looks doing it last night but the fact that you were no longer *quite* the heiress you were before.' Now a small significant laugh.

'You say some strange things,' observed Zenith.

'But pertinent?'

'. . . Would you say them to—Dad?'

'No. But you wouldn't, either. I sized you up at once. You obviously didn't like me, but you would still never hurt your father. You're soft, Zenith, a nice attribute no doubt, but there's no room for softness in the world today.' A pause. 'That goes for the lovesick Helen as well.'

'Helen?' Zenith queried.

'She'd die at the stake for Derek, wouldn't she?' drawled Carol.

'I—I don't know.'

'Then *know*. But I've had enough of women's conversation. I'll go and visit the good Brent, seeing you don't object.' Carol went calmly through the doorway and down the street.

Shaken, Zenith returned to her small-time world of finger painting, sand castles, rides on the swing, the rest. I never thought, she was realising hollowly, that I would have preferred subtleties, evasions and deceits to truth. But I know now that I do. I prefer them to *Carol's* brand of truth.

She was still shaken when the mothers came out of their classes and crossed to the nursery to collect their treasures. Some of them had husbands off duty this afternoon, and undoubtedly they would make for the hot artesian springs some ten miles out where the boss had provided a picnic and barbecue area. The others would seek out the tennis courts, or form happy gossipy groups down at the trading post.

Meanwhile Zenith's chore was over. She was free.

A little unsteadily, though she hoped not showing it, Zenith bade goodbye to the last of her children and their mums, then left the nursery school in a manner that was strictly forbidden, especially to the boss's daughter, since the boss and his daughter were always expected to do the right and correct thing, to be an example.

In short, Zenith went without her protective helmet.

It would not have mattered if she had gone straight home, but she did not. Absently she wandered down the track towards the Cut.

There were many open cuts at Savage, but when one spoke of the Cut they meant *this* cut, the first cut of all, the one surrounded (and very unfortunately) by the town that had cropped up, and the biggest of them all.

The Cut was positively immense. When you stood on the platform provided and looked down, you could not believe it, it was too gargantuan, too unreal. There were weaving roads snaking round the steep cliff sides of it, and up and down these tracks crawled yellow ants ... jeeps, lorries, some occasional tournarockers. The tournarockers were the soldier ants, Zenith always thought.

Then there were the dots of men, no shape, no man

semblance at all, simply pinpoints of yellow again. The yellow was their safety helmets, the helmet ... and still Zenith did not realise it ... that she had left behind her at the school.

For the rest, there was just a hole, a vast gaping hole. Yellow ants, yellow dots, twisting tracks and a hole: that was the Cut.

Zenith looked down bemused.

It should have been hideously ugly, a gaping wound had to be that, but the purple aura of the ore had clothed it and made it almost a beautiful thing. The mauve air persisted everywhere. Zenith leaned out instinctively to entrap it in her hands, as children try to entrap sky, and that was the last she remembered before she felt herself sliding down and out. Too late she realised that in her abstraction she had left the safety viewing platform and looked down instead from where she, and everyone else, was forbidden to look. Now she was slipping to destruction, it had to be destruction from such a height, and unless some miracle happened ...

The miracle happened on the third snake from the top, the track only wide enough to take the wheels of ascending or descending vehicles, not a bare inch more. The flattened space should have been enough to delay Zenith, and it might have had she not had the acceleration of the descent behind her. Nevertheless she still tried desperately. She tensed herself painfully against the awful downward slide again, she resisted, she held back ... then the fingers caught her.

She supposed with a lucidity that surprised her ... how could she be lucid after all this? ... that fingers they must be. There was no shrub or bush or anything to pull her back, not in the Cut. The Cut was completely bare.

The fingers held, they grabbed, clamped and trapped, then slowly, agonisingly for Zenith, they began to tug her back.

It took all Steve Forbuck's strength to break the fall, to stop himself from falling with the girl. But he did stop her, and even after all danger was over he still held her, held her with a hard tightness that made the agony of that first delaying grasp of his almost a trivial act in contrast.

Zenith gasped in the iron-hard control, then when after several minutes it still did not relax, she began to try to withdraw. After all, a rescue was a rescue, but when it persisted ...

But Steve still held her, held her punitively, a little brutally, then slowly at last he let her go. Exhausted, they both lay back.

The man recovered first.

'Where's your helmet?' he demanded.

'It's not on my head,' Zenith retorted pertly.

'I didn't ask you that.'

'I'm sorry, I meant I wasn't wearing it because I left it behind me at the school.'

'You knew you should wear it?'

'Oh, yes.'

'Then?'

'I just didn't,' she said wretchedly. 'Anyhow' ... brightening ... 'there's been no need.'

Even as she uttered it there was a tumble of loose rocks from above. At once he pulled her to him, put his own helmet on her head.

'No need?' he asked her.

The little landslide stopped. Shakily Zenith disciplined herself to look down. The yellow ants were still moving around. One of the larger yellow ants, the soldier ants, not the tournarocker but still almost as big a truck, was beginning the snaky ascent to the top.

'Do you think they noticed us?' she asked sensitively, very aware of her shortcomings. 'Down there, I mean.'

'Noticed *you*, I think you're trying to say. *I* have no qualms at being noticed; I was not out of my place, and I was correctly dressed. But no, I don't think you were noticed. It's rather a long way, you see.'

'Yes.' Zenith shivered.

'You haven't told me why yet,' he demanded, 'why you came out in regulation *un*dress. Why you came here at all. Why you left the viewing platform. You don't seem like that to me.'

'Like what?'

'Reckless. Foolhardy. Rather you seem the boss's daughter.'

'Is that bad?' she asked.

'I'm not saying so.'

'Then is it good?'

'Rather let us say a good example ... or should be.'

'Yes,' agreed Zenith ashamedly, 'and I generally try to show a good example. Dad expects it. Or' ... she bit her lip ... 'he *has* expected it.'

'So you're going to make that your excuse now, are you? Say that your father no longer expects it of you? Not now that he——'

'Not now that he——?' asked Zenith piteously.

'Not now that he has someone else on his plate apart from his precious daughter,' he said laconically.

'Yes—Carol. His fiancée.'

'Exactly,' he agreed.

A few moments went by.

'You did know her before, didn't you?' Zenith probed.

He did not answer.

'She came up here after you.'

'*That* she did *not*. She came after bigger fish than I could ever be.'

'It didn't appear so last night,' she said drily.

'So you were interested in us?'

He raised his eyebrows.

'I had to see the two of you. Everyone had to.'

'Then I can tell you that you at least were looking with jaundiced eyes.'

'Eyes for Dad,' Zenith defended. 'I can't and I won't have him hurt.'

'If by that you mean that Carol won't go through with things because of me, you're wrong, my dear.'

'I said hurt, not unmarried. Also I'm not your dear.'

'Brent's?'

'No.'

'But you have to be someone's.' He spoke idly. 'In a remote project like Savage it's an expected thing.'

'Was it expected in your last project? The project where you met Carol? Was she your——'

' "My dear"? Oh, no.'

'Then were you hers?'

'Possibly. You must have noticed how fascinating I am.'

'No,' said Zenith flatly.

'But you haven't been unaware of me?' he suggested slyly.

She went to deny that, then decided instead on truth.

'How could I be unaware when you've abused me ever since the moment we met?'

'If you call holding you from certain death a few moments ago abuse, then yes.'

'I might have been in danger, but did the rescue need to be that—well, that——'

'Yes. That. And now be quiet for a few moments, boss's daughter. There's a truck about to turn the corner ... no, don't slink back, there's not even room for that. We're catching it.'

'Catching it?' she queried.

'It will be climbing dead slow ... naturally. I'll shove you up beside the driver then haul myself among the ore.'

'I can't let you do that,' Zenith protested.

'Then how do you propose to get out of here?'

Zenith looked down at the almost perpendicular descent, up at the almost perpendicular ascent. He was right. They could have been perched on a cliff top the way they were situated, it was either join whatever came up or went down, or fall and be crushed.

'We could try walking,' she said uncertainly.

'Crawling, you mean, and you can, but I won't. There's too much traffic today for my liking.' He pointed to a veritable string of ants below and above waiting to make the journey. 'Here comes our chance. Look at the driver's surprised face! He certainly didn't anticipate being thumbed here.' As he was saying it, Steve Forbuck was swinging Zenith off her feet and pushing her through a window, he was standing back, flatter, Zenith thought, than a shadow, back from the big wheels only a fraction from his toes. He waited until the truck had laboured past, then he swung himself aloft among the spoil. The ant proceeded round the turns of the hole, and at last reached the top. Here the driver stopped to let Zenith out, and in the brief halt Steve Forbuck jumped down from the back and took her place in the cabin.

Zenith supposed she should say Thank You to someone, but though she tried, no words came.

When at last she did find a small voice, the truck and the men had left.

CHAPTER FOUR

WHEN Zenith got to the boss's house it was to find Carol standing on the verandah, and obviously in a very bad mood.

It was unbelievable how a scowl took away every vestige of her remarkable beauty; she looked an unattractive and unpleasant young woman. Too late Zenith remembered her own role of hostess. She should have come straight home and been here awaiting Carol's return from Brent's office, she should not have wandered abstractedly to the Cut as she had. But too late now, the thing was done.

'Where in Betsy have you been?' Carol burst irritably.

'I'm sorry, Carol, but I thought that Brent——'

'Your friend did suggest a bite at the canteen, but I fancied something a little choosier than canteen stuff.'

'Then you know canteen stuff,' Zenith flashed.

Carol gave her a sharp look but did not answer her. Instead she resumed with her complaint.

'I came back here hoping that the expert Pierre ... was that the name? ... might rustle me up something choosier than what the canteen could offer, and what do I find? An empty kitchen.'

'It was also empty this morning,' Zenith pointed out.

'That didn't matter—I never eat breakfast. But the wretched cook still isn't there. Where is he?'

In a small voice Zenith said: 'Gone.' She followed it at once with: 'Please forgive me. I should have told you before.'

'Told me what?'

'That we have now no personal cook.'

Carol was silent a moment, an angry silence going by the tightness of her mouth. 'Yes, you should have,' she said at length. 'So should your father.' 'Your father', not Derek, not any of the fond, personal names a future wife usually adopts for her husband-to-be. Zenith winced.

'Father didn't know,' she defended.

'Know what?'

'What I'm telling you—that Pierre has left us. On your plane in, as a matter of fact. Yesterday's.' A sigh. 'It was the Champignons that did it.'

'The what? Oh, you are a stupid girl!'

Carol turned on her heel and went down the hall, Zenith behind her.

'What have I come to?' Carol was asking bitterly. 'A madhouse?'

'Perhaps it seems like that, but——'

'No perhaps, it *is*. I arrive last night to a red carpet and this morning find bare floors.'

'It's all bare floors,' misinterpreted Zenith, 'no one goes in for carpet up here.'

'I wasn't speaking literally, of course. Really, you *are* stupid!' Once more Carol said it. 'I arrived to— to—— Oh, what's the use of telling *you*? But the fact remains, it's quite intolerable. I have half a mind to——'

'To leave?' The two words were out before Zenith could stop them. She clapped her hand over her mouth.

'Oh, no,' said Carol smoothly and at once, 'not that.' She was smiling blandly again. 'It's only a storm in a teacup,' she went on smoothly. 'Let's forget it. Just make me some coffee and sandwiches, dear. That will do. And don't dread telling your father' ... 'your father' again! ... 'that you're incapable of running his domestic affairs, for I'll do that for you. In a nice manner, of course. Well, why not? We're all one nice family, aren't we ... or soon will be.'

'*How* soon, Carol?' Zenith could hardly recognise her own disliking voice.

Carol shrugged her lovely shoulders; she had conquered her bad temper and was exquisitely, calmly beautiful again.

'Quite soon,' she promised.

'I think Dad would like a project wedding,' said Zenith, deciding to be as calm if not so beautiful herself. 'Our Reverend William Flett——'

'Who's he?'

'Savage's own inland flying pastor.'

'How quaint! And what is it you were thinking?'

'That you and Dad—that you——'

'I see. Definitely not. No, we'll be married in Sydney, of course. St Mark's. Coffee ready yet?'

'Coming,' Zenith said in a strangled kind of voice.

Derek Smith arrived at the same time as his daughter poured Carol's second cup. He smiled happily as he saw the two girls sitting ostensibly companionably together. Poor Dad, Zenith thought, he wants everything as cosy as—well, as it's *not*.—And never will be. Zenith felt sure of that.

'A pretty sight,' Derek beamed. 'One there for me, Zennie?'

'Of course, Dad.'

'Yes, but not brewed by Pierre,' Carol told him with a pretty pout. 'Naughty boy, you should have told me.' She touched Derek's hand.

'My dear?' Derek was plainly puzzled.

In spite of Carol's decision that *she* would tell him, Zenith broke in first.

'Pierre has gone,' she blurted. 'My fault, Dad. He asked for—— Oh, what does it matter? He still went.'

'Been intending to all along, no doubt,' Derek nodded understandingly, understanding for his daughter. 'But when? How long ago?'

'Yesterday.'

'Yet what about last night's very worthy meal?'

'Helen did it,' said Zenith flatly.

'Yes, Derek, the good Helen.' It was Carol, sweetly and sincerely . . . and for Dad's benefit.

'Yes, indeed, Carol, Helen is very good. So our Helen came to the rescue. I must thank her for that.'

'I wouldn't,' advised Carol. 'It might embarrass her. Good by stealth and all that.'

'But——'

'I know women,' Carol assured him, and Derek smiled and shrugged.

'I suppose you're right, dear.'

'I am.'

. . . You're not, though, Zenith thought. Helen would have appreciated thanks from Dad, to Helen it would have been——

'How will we manage without Pierre?' Derek looked regretfully at Carol.

'It's nothing,' smiled Carol. 'I'll try my hand, and then there's always the canteen.' Impossible to think that only a few moments ago she had shuddered at the canteen.

'You won't mind, Carol?'

'So long as you look at me across the table,' smiled Carol.

Derek leaned over and touched her hand.

'Thank heaven for a co-operative crew,' he said after he had taken his hand away. 'At least' ... a frown now ... 'I thought they were co-operative.'

Both girls looked at the boss.

'It has been reported to me that there was a head to-day without a helmet,' Derek went on.

'Mine,' said Carol. 'I walked up to see Zenith's school.'

'*Not* you, dear, and though I recommend helmets at all times, I very much doubt if you'd come to any harm walking bareheaded up there. But don't do it again.'

'I wouldn't have done it the first time if I'd been told, or if I'd been given a helmet.' Carol hung her head prettily.

'You weren't told?' Derek turned to his daughter. 'Really, Zennie——'

Zenith bit her lip, but did not defend herself. Anyway, what could she have said? She had *not* warned Carol.

'However, it was not you I was referring to, Carol,' Derek continued, 'I doubt if anyone would report a bareheaded girl in the town. No, this girl was at—the Cut.'

'Me,' Zenith said resignedly.

'Yes, I know, I was told so, but I still couldn't believe it.'

'Told by your new man, no doubt,' said Zenith bitterly.

'He was doing his duty,' her father pointed out.

'And enjoying doing it.'

'Really, Zenith, I don't know what's got into you. You've always been as keen as I am to set a good example. How in heaven did you come to do such a damn fool thing?'

Zenith sighed. 'I wasn't thinking.'

'Obviously. And not thinking, either, when you didn't put out a helmet for Carol. Get one now.'

Zenith rose. She was rankling under the unaccustomed note of dissatisfaction and the ring of authority in her father's voice; he had never used quite such a tone to her before. Yet it wasn't Dad's fault really, it was Carol's for drawing Dad's attention to his daughter's omissions.—Most of all it was *his* fault. The Pig's fault.

She found a helmet and came and handed it to Carol.

Carol put it on, and—well, it just wasn't fair. The strictly utilitarian thing did strictly un-utilitarian things to Carol. She looked . . . glorious. The yellow, barely a shade deeper than her moon-blonde hair, brought out the creamy perfection of her skin, made her blue eyes bluer. Zenith saw her father's own eyes widening, then shining as he gazed proudly at her in possessive admiration. It was quite a while before he could look away again.

Carol, aware of the picture she had made, got up like a good little girl and said she would put the helmet on her dressing table to remind her always to wear it.

When she had gone, Zenith mumbled: 'Sorry, Dad.'

'Sorry, too, Zennie, I didn't mean to bawl you out. Actually I was worried about you. How did you happen to do it?'

'You mean wander to the Cut?'

He nodded.

'I just wandered,' she shrugged.

'Without thinking? That's not like you.'

... Oh, I was thinking, Zenith could have said. Aloud she mumbled: 'I'm truly sorry, Dad.'

'All right, let it pass.'

'You say that, Dad, but you don't look it.'—Dad didn't, there was a concern somewhere there in him that her apology had not removed.

'You mean I don't look like letting it pass?' He smiled, but somehow the smile didn't come off. 'Then you're right, Zen, I don't look it, because—well——'

'Yes, Dad?'

'I have a little worry.'

Zenith held her breath. Carol? she wondered. If she had been honest she would have said *hoped*.

But no, it was not that.

'You've heard, of course, about the floodwaters that have isolated Big Billy?'—Big Billy was an oil rig some six hundred kilometres north-west.

'Yes, Dad.'

'Well, the waters are on the move, Zenith.'

'On the move?' she echoed.

'They're leaving the rig,' he explained.

'You mean drying up?'

'I don't mean that, I mean getting away.' He looked at Zenith keenly. 'Good for Billy—but bad for someone else?'

'Someone else?'

'Us.'

'Us?' she echoed.

'Yes.'

'But we couldn't be flooded here, Dad. Why, we never even see any rain! The biggest fall we ever had was a scant——'

'Not rain, Zen, water. Water on the move. And the only move is to Savage. We're the only natural, the only feasible drainage for Billy. Steve and I have gone through it again and again.'

'Steve and you?' she queried.

'Yes. Forbuck.'

'And what would he know?'

'A whole lot, I hope, the subject is what he came for.'

'The subject ... what subject? Forbuck's just a Category: Manual working through the different aspects to better himself, isn't he?' Zenith could not stop herself adding: 'Or hoping to.'

Fortunately in his absorption her father did not hear her, so she amended quickly: 'But, Dad, that could be awful! The cuts could be ruined.'

Derek Smith shrugged. 'It would certainly be a setback, but not necessarily a disaster. The holes would still produce afterwards, the spoil would still be present.

'But if it happens, what do I do? That is what is concerning me, Zenith, bringing my worried frown.'

'I think you mean what do you do with the staff?'

'Yes. We could be completely isolated. If we followed Big Billy's example it could be an isolation for anything up to three months, even more. What will the men say when I tell them?'

'You mean you're intending to let them know all this?'

'Of course. If I tell them they could decide if they prefer to leave here now, or stay on till the last moment. Then you, Zen, you would have to make up your mind.'

'It's made already,' she assured him. 'This is home.'

'Then—Carol.' Derek Smith had risen and had walked to the other end of the room. Although his back was turned on her, Zenith could sense the uncertainty in him. the need for confidence, the need for——

'But Carol would never leave,' Zenith said at once. 'She would never leave you, Dad.'

'No. No.' He had turned again and he was smiling at Zenith, smiling at her reassurance. 'And you, dear,' he grinned. 'Apart from being besotted with the place, would you, in Carol's position, stay on for the man you love?'

The man she loved. Zenith sat very still, aware suddenly of an odd thumping somewhere inside of her. The man she loved. But she loved no man.

She was grateful that she did not have to answer the question, even jocularly. Carol came back into the room and crossed and slipped her hand into Derek's. Presently they both went out.

But Zenith went and stood at the window, trying to imagine encircling waters, all the cuts inundated with yellow flood.

It wouldn't happen. Forbuck was an agitator. Dad was just being cautious, he had always been cautious, cautious in everything but——

But the girl he loved, for girl was all Carol was compared to Dad. Spring and autumn, it worked out often, but could it work now ... and could it work if what Dad had just told her took place? Flood isolation meant so much more than just water everywhere. It meant inconvenience, rationing, discomfort, dismalness, the

same people beside you every minute of every day, it
meant monotony. If you loved someone, then that was
all right. But *did* Carol ... *did* she ...

'Would you stay on for the man you love?' she heard
her father asking again ... and again she felt that dis-
tinct, inexplicable thump of her heart. She got up and
went out to the kitchen. She had no idea of what she
could produce for a meal, and she simply could not ask
Helen again, but at least she knew the steaks must be
defrosted.

She took the meat out of the freezer, crying in pain
at the cruel cold on her bare hands, then she stood looking at it, not realising she was not seeing it at all, not
seeing anything, just looking blankly.

Oh, Dad, she was thinking, don't get hurt.

As was only to be expected with meat so long in deep
freeze, the steaks were white and stiff. Too late Zenith
remembered how Pierre always had defrosted over-
night, done it with distaste, for, like all his countrymen,
he abhorred any food that was not freshly marketed,
then promptly cooked. Looking at the stiff white
boards, Zenith shared his disgust, but was more disgusted still, when, after pouring boiling water (not the
best defrosting method, she knew) over the meat, it did
at last unbend, but achieved the unbending in a very
unappetising manner. Where the hot water touched, it
bleached, and where it didn't, it bled.

'Yuk!' Carol, who had returned, had come out to the
kitchen, and stood grimacing at the steaks.

'I did intend to take over,' Carol shuddered, 'but I
certainly couldn't try my special secret on a mess like
that.'

'Then it will have to be a tin,' shrugged Zenith.

'No, the canteen,' Carol said promptly, putting a strand of hair into place. She did not seem at all put out at the idea. 'What time do the boys eat?'

'By boys I presume you mean the single men. They eat when they go to the canteen.' It was presumptuous, but Zenith still said it, and Carol did not bat an eyelid.

'But you must know whether they eat early or late . . . oh, it doesn't matter. We'll go, anyway, and sit over a bottle of white wine.'

'It's a dry canteen,' Zenith told her.

'But there's a bar.'

'Not in the dining room.'

'Then the boss will have to show his rank, won't he? He'll have to take a bottle in.'

'I don't think Dad will.'

'Dad mightn't, but I believe Derek might.' A pause. 'Isn't it time you stopped thinking of him as Dad, Zenith?'

'He is my father,' Zenith pointed out.

'I really meant . . . and you know it . . . stop thinking of him in that childish way. You are, after all, little younger than I am. An adult.'

A minute went by in silence. Then Zenith said: 'I think halfway between early and late should be about right.' She added: 'For the canteen.' She turned and went out of the kitchen.

The boss arrived home soon after, and was plainly disappointed at the prospect of a meal in the canteen when he had anticipated something much more personal.

'Sorry, Dad.' Again Zenith had to say it. 'The steak wouldn't defrost.'

'Not exactly right, it defrosted too much,' corrected

Carol with a shudder. 'Poor dear' ... she touched Derek's arm ... 'tomorrow perhaps?'

'With you at the helm?' he smiled.

'I promise.'

Again Zenith turned away.

The three of them strolled up to the canteen at seven o'clock. Zenith saw that the men, the two of them, anyhow, who might interest Carol, had already arrived, and she was thankful for that, since the selection on the blackboard offered either stewed chops or stewed steak, a choice she knew would scarcely excite Carol. However, the men helped the situation, Brent with his eager acknowledgment of the female company, Steve with his deliberate ... and tantalising ... uninterest, even if the presence of Helen as well was not to Carol's liking.

'Does that woman always eat here?' she demanded in a not-too-quiet voice. 'Always tag along?'

Tag along? Helen?

'The single people do eat here,' Zenith said stiffly, 'only the married and family ones eat at home.'

'Something she hasn't achieved yet,' said Carol nastily.

'What do you mean, Carol?'

'Marriage. Though not, I would say, for the want of trying.'

'*I* wouldn't say that,' retorted Zenith.

'Wouldn't you?'

'No. They ... the men ... are all younger than Helen.'

'... Your father?'

'*You* are marrying Father.'

'What is this marriage talk? What have I missed?' Derek, whose attention had been on something else, turned round now and smiled at them both.

'I'm sorry, Carol,' he went on before either of the girls could tell him, though, of course, they wouldn't, 'that we still haven't overcome our own food question. I would wire at once for a cook, but—well, to tell you the truth——'

'They're hard to come by?' helped Carol magnanimously. Obviously she was feeling magnanimous, Brent's open admiration would have done that to anyone.

'I'm really thinking *unfair* to come by.'

'I understand, Derek. You mean a cook wouldn't be needed long because we wouldn't be here long, is that it?' Carol said sweetly.

'No—no, I didn't mean quite that either. Look, Carol dear, there's something you must know. I told Zen earlier.'

'Yet not me.' A pretty little pout.

'It was only concern for you that stopped me. It's this: I'm expecting . . . perhaps anticipating would be a better word . . . a—a——'

'Yes, Derek?'

The boss took out a notebook and pencil and began sketching the position of the Big Billy oil rig, and the water there, and how when . . . if . . . it moved, it would have to move to Savage.

'Meaning,' he said honestly, 'we would be inundated.'

'Surrounded by water?'

'An island, Carol.'

'No one in, no one out?'

'That's it exactly, dear. That's why I wouldn't like to tie a new man up, not when I was aware of what could happen. It will be bad enough, if it happens, tying the old lot up. Oh, I'd give my boys their choice of staying or getting out, but for those who elected to remain it would still be a tie.'

'But you'd tie me up?' Carol said at once, and Zenith gave her a quick incredulous look; she had expected an outburst at least from Carol, certainly no loving acceptance as the girl was showing now.

'Well, dear,' Derek said, 'it would be your choice.'

'I've made it.'

'Yes, Carol?'

'I've made my choice. We' ... Carol paused for good effect ... 'had better get married straight away, hadn't we, Derek?' She flashed Zenith the briefest of triumphant glances, so brief she might not have looked at all. 'Because, dear,' she went on, 'if we're to be enclosed here——'

Zenith sat nonplussed. All her previous doubts about Carol seemed confounded. The girl was not playing Dad along, she was not accepting him only for his money, solely with the intention of city living and no place else, she was serious, so serious she would accept what could ... and might ... lie ahead. Now Dad only had to say the eager word and——

Then an unexpected thing happened, unexpected, anyway, by Zenith. She simply could not believe her father's measured reply.

'No, I don't think I want it like that, Carol. I brought you up here to make quite sure, remember? I want it slower, dear girl, I want it more certain. That's why I insisted on you looking around here first, more importantly getting to know me better first. We're spring and autumn, don't forget, and autumn can wait.' A smile at Carol. 'Can spring?'

'Of course, Derek.' Again Carol said it at once. There was nothing at all to be read in her lovely face, neither impatience nor disappointment, and if she had lost a point, she gave no sign.

So she does intend to marry him. Zenith looked at the canteen blackboard but saw only a blur of white chalk. I should be thankful for that at least, she thought, thankful that Carol understands, and is compliant. I should be thankful that Dad isn't being too headstrong, too—too——

Too cautious? Derek said 'certain', but isn't it really 'cautious'? And why? Why is Dad being deliberate like this? Love is never deliberate, or it shouldn't **be**. There should be no second thoughts.

She glanced from the blurred blackboard and saw her father's hand reaching out to enclose Carol's.

She looked away at once, not so impelled by a wish not to see as a curious feeling that she was being watched herself.

She was. Across from the next table, staring quite openly at her, Steve Forbuck nodded at her, and then, hatefully, impertinently, he winked. The wink was because of Carol and her father, and it was knowing ... and amused.

CHAPTER FIVE

LIFE went on in the days that followed as though there was no massive withdrawal of water beginning from the Big Billy rig, as though the large left-over from the last rains that had isolated Billy for months was not seeping south. Life went on as it always went at Savage ... changeover whistles, wives exchanging confidences at the school, at the trading post, everywhere they met. The spoil was still wrested from Mother Earth, and there were still little yellow ants working in the cuts.

The orchestra met as it always did, and the boss's party, including Helen, Brent and now Steve, also met and danced.

Even the annual Cooee Trial was staged the same as last year.

The Cooee event was not strictly an inland tradition, it had been adopted from Queensland, from which, anyway, most of these hard red men came. The Trial consisted of a Cooee (the Australian bushman's call) Competition, Cattle Singing, even though, with the arrival of the miners, the cattle perforce had left, and Kookaburra Laughing, also not a sound now heard at Savage, since kookaburras had to have trees, and what trees had once struggled here in the desert had given way to the demands of the cuts.

Yet hold it Savage did, even with the prospect of descending waters threatening them, and every evening aspiring cooee callers, cattle singers or kookaburra laughers tried out their voice power from Savage's sole 'high rise', known as Wreck Mountain, an incline so meagre it had to be specially indicated to the new-comer. The rules were that the call or the song or the laugh had to be plainly heard for a quarter of a mile.

Quality counted, too. The 'coo' of the 'cooee' had to be long and musical and the 'ee' high-pitched, the cattle singing guaranteed to put the crankiest beast to sleep, and the kookaburra laugh startle the hawks and harriers, which, with a few ground birds, comprised all the feathered life out here, into thinking that old jackass was back again.

To top it all the miners had arranged a beer-drinking contest, and the reigning champion was taking on all comers, his time for a twenty-ounce glass standing at four seconds.

'It's disgusting!' Carol burst out.

'Yes, I agree,' nodded Zenith, 'but it only happens once a year.'

Carol did not say anything, but her eyes flicked: '*My* last year' as clearly as if she had declared it aloud.

The situation between Carol and her father con-tinually puzzled Zenith. Since that night at the canteen when Dad had firmly refused the early marriage offer that Carol had made to him Zenith had had to change her mind over the spring–autumn affair. Before that she had seen Carol only as a cunning manipulator, but now she was unsure. It had been Dad instead who had manipulated, he had manoeuvred a stay in the proceed-ings, and the girl had presumably been genuine after all.

Right from the beginning Zenith had suspected that Carol had been playing Dad along for something, using him, and yet it had been Carol who had acted frankly, her father who had not. It could be that Dad had wanted his young fiancée to be quite sure, as he had said, but should love be so organised? Even when autumn was dealing with spring, and time out for thinking indicated, should it? Zenith had no answer.

Zenith's feeling, too, that Carol had only gone into the affair with Dad's top rank in view had later been damned by Carol's calm acceptance of the loss Derek Smith would certainly incur if the rig waters isolated them. For a brief moment when Zenith once mentioned this fact to Carol, Carol had seemed shocked, but the reaction had been very brief, barely a reaction at all.

'You say it would disadvantage Derek?' she asked.

'It would be a big setback.'

'I see.'

But that had been all.

One early evening Zenith drove out in the Rover to a spot beyond Wreck Mountain to hear the cooee callers, the cattle singers and the kookaburra laughers practise their bit, for the trial date was close now.

She was used to the terrain by now, as accustomed as if she had been born to it. The sudden man-made hills of waste, two of them reaching over twenty metres, no longer surprised her; she did not wonder, as newcomers did, if she had travelled by some time capsule into another planet. For it was rather like visiting the moon, Zenith thought, everything rock-strewn, dust-encased, bare except for the inevitable spinifex.

Yet the excavations gaping widely beside the waste hills had known much more excitement than any moonscape. In each hole machines had roared, trucks had shuttled away precious spoil, and many workers, those yellow men ants, had toiled. Some had even died.

Now the depleted holes were left like unhealed wounds, but restoration would be undertaken, even out here at Savage where possibly no visitor would ever come restoration would be carefully applied, it was her father's most urgent policy, and because open-cut mining was more humane, much safer, Zenith looked at it all with a more tolerant eye than she ordinarily would. She glanced at her speedometer, reckoned she had covered a quarter mile, and drew up the Rover. Now to hear the cooee callers, the cattle singers, the kookaburra laughers.

She sat very still in the jeep.

'Coo-ee!' There went one, but not at all distinctly. He shouldn't win, Zenith judged. A singer tried out a few bars, a kookaburra chortled, then clearly came two syllables again. Cooee! No, it was not cooee, it was— why, it was——

It was Zen-ith. Zen-ith!

What nonsense was this?

Angry at having her name called over the public address system, as it were, Zenith got firmly out of the jeep, her lips set.

'Zen-ith!' There it came again. And it came clearly. Too clearly. The wretched caller might not have the right message, but he certainly did have the right penetrating lungs.

'Zen-ith!'

Zenith walked to the edge of Wreck Mountain and looked back to Savage. She looked with distaste. There was only one person she knew who would call deliberately and impertinently like that. Certainly none of the old hands would, they thought too much of her. How dared he make a laughing stock of her? How dared Steve Forbuck?

It was at that moment she saw Steve emerging from a thicket of mulga that must have escaped the tree barbering that cuts entailed, and she understood why he had been so clear. He had not been calling out a required quarter of a mile away, he had been calling from no more than a hundred yards. She should have felt relieved that her name was not being bandied around, but she only felt angrier still. This man, this wretched man ...

He was approaching her now, coming in that assured way of his, sure that she would still be there. Well, to spite him she wouldn't. There was no time to return to the jeep, get it started and get back, but there was time to turn on one's heel and go in the opposite direction.

That was what Zenith did ... for exactly six steps.

Then she fell, fell without warning. If she had had a moment to think about it she would have mused that she was making quite a habit of falling lately.

There was not much to fall from at Wreck Mountain, but though it was a meagre rise, all the height happened steeply and at once. It also happened in mud. There must have been an old wurlie or watering hole in the vicinity, for in a world of dryness the sharp slope was surfaced with black squelch.

Zenith toppled over, fell into a first bog of mud, bounced, fell into a second mound of mud, then finally reached the bottom, still mud. She was lying there, too disgusted with herself to move, when Steve Forbuck slid down to her. The first thing she noticed, apart from his grin, was that he had remained clean. Why should he emerge so immaculate? she fumed. She tried to sit up.

But she had forgotten how mud can grab. It grabbed now at Zenith and imprisoned her. Perhaps she had struck quicksands; she had never heard of any out here, but there still could be some. The thoughts of sinking to death in black mire brought the beginnings of a scream to her lips.

'Ease up,' her rescuer drawled. 'The competition hasn't started yet, and if that sound is intended to sing the cattle asleep ...' Steve Forbuck in his careful slide down had escaped the patches of mud, and he spoke with assurance now from a dry position some feet from Zenith. He extended his hand to drag her across to the clean patch, and though she wanted to resist Zenith took his hand and accepted his help. She was sick of slush.

She must have muttered so, because he shook his head. 'Slush could have saved your life, though. Yes, I mean that. There's rock here, too, sharp rock, but because of the cushioning mire you've missed it. So give thanks for glorious mud.'

'It's ruined my clothes,' she snapped, 'and who knows it wasn't quicksand mud, the kind that sucks you in and smothers you.'

'Inch by inch,' he nodded, 'your nose the last of you.' He had looked around and actually found a dry twig, though from where in this wilderness Zenith did not know. He tossed the twig in the mud he had just pulled her from, and waited. The twig sat there undisturbed on top of the squelch.

'See, no quicksand,' he grinned. 'Therefore no dis-

appearing nose, which, in your instance' ... he scrutin-
ised her ... 'wouldn't take long.'

'You like sculptured features, then? Like Carol's?'

'How did she come into this?'

'She didn't ... I mean ...'

'You don't know what you mean in this muddy
moment. Feel like climbing up again yet?'

'Yes,' Zenith said, though movement was the last
thing she wanted. She felt dizzy from the unexpected
tumble, grazed, bruised, and, she suspected, slightly
concussed.

He was on his feet beside her now, pulling her up.
But when she swayed involuntarily he lowered her
down again.

'Liar,' he accused, 'you're "shook up", and won't admit it.'

'Give me five minutes.'

'I'll give you the rest of my life, Zenith.' Either he
said that or he said the rest of your life; Zenith did not
know. She had closed her eyes to let the world spin
round her and the words were unclear. But of course,
they would be the rest of *your* life, her own life, as it
entailed him, did not interest Steve Forbuck.

The reaction did not last long. Slowly everything
straightened, and so did Zenith.

She got to her feet.

He helped her climb up, but when they reached the
top instead of veering her to her jeep ... evidently he
had walked over, for she could see no other car ... he
headed her to a small rock cleft.

'Water,' he indicated, '*clean* water. I suspect its spill-
over is what keeps the mud remaining mud. I thought
you might like to clean up before you went back. Mire
can be embarrassing.'

'Yes. Thank you.' She followed him to the tiny catchment.

But when they reached there, the caught-up water was too high for her to reach, so Steve took out a big handkerchief, wet it, then began the cleaning up process by hand.

He made a fair job of it, and Zenith was reluctantly grateful. She would have hated returning in such a state.

'I'm sorry I caused you all this trouble.' At least Zenith felt she should say that.

Steve Forbuck did not answer at once, and had Zenith looked at him she would have disbelieved what she saw: a tenderness. But, sensitively, Zenith was looking away.

'Yes,' said the man, 'it has been a trouble.' He paused in his sponging. 'Why?'

'Why?' she queried.

'Why did you run away from me, Miss Smith, for that's how you fell.'

'I—I didn't want to see you.'

'Why, again?'

Zenith stared wordlessly ahead of her, suddenly aware of something, not wanting to be aware of it, but —*aware*. She had run away because— because——

'I'm waiting,' Steve Forbuck said grimly.

But Zenith gave no answer. How could she answer? How could she say to this man: 'I didn't want to see you because you arrived here at the same time as Carol, and nothing will ever convince me that that was not intentional, either on her part or yours. If it was on Carol's part, then it makes this thing that she's pretending for Dad a travesty, and though I don't mind that, not wanting and not liking her, I do mind Dad being hurt. But if coming here after Carol is your move, then——'

Then I'm hurt as well.

Zenith gave a sudden shiver. It was as if the words had been said for her, and the impact of them rocked her. Just as she had been shaken that day Derek had asked her was there anyone to keep her tied here at Savage during a flood, she was shaken now.

'Someone walk over your grave?' Steve said it casually, but there was a probing there. 'Is answering a simple question that bad?'

'Wh-what did you ask me?'

'You know damn well, you little liar. I asked you why you didn't want to see me.'

'I expect because I'd sooner see other people,' she avoided.

'Davids?'

'No.'

'Who then?'

'I don't know. Can we go back, please?'

'It's your car,' he shrugged.

'You walked over?'

'Yes.'

'Then can I take you back?'

'No.'

'Then can you take me? You see, I'm still a bit shaken.'

Steve Forbuck looked at Zenith narrowly. 'It wasn't all that much of a fall.'

'The mud——' she began.

'Mud never shook anyone up yet. No, Zenith, I do believe you were—pre-shaken.'

'Pre-shaken?' she echoed.

'Shaken before Wreck Mountain. Not your usual self, though what your usual self is I wouldn't know. Anyway, the tumble simply clinched it. What's the matter? Things getting you down?'

'No. People.'

'You're people, too. As a matter of interest, what kind of people were you once upon a time?'

'The usual, I expect,' she shrugged.

'With a name as soaring as Zenith? Oh, no.'

'I think my parents were very happy about me,' Zenith explained of her name.

'And now one of them is gone,' he said quietly, with gentleness.

'I can't even remember her,' said Zenith. 'But I've always been proud of my happy name, happy for Dad's happiness. At least, Dad's happiness until——'

'Until?'

But Zenith had set her lips.

'A man can't live on memories for ever,' Steve Forbuck reminded her levelly, and Zenith knew he was referring to her father and what was happening to him after many years.

'I didn't want Dad to,' she defended, 'I never wanted anything lonely or empty for Dad, but I didn't want, and I don't want——' Again she set her lips.

'You didn't want a Carol?'

'No.'

'Was there anyone you did want?' he asked shrewdly.

'Yes.'

'I see. Then we both have a same thing: a want.' He said it unexpectedly, and Zenith turned and looked at him.

'A want?' she asked.

'Yes.'

'So you did come after Carol?'

'No.'

'You just said——'

'I said we both had a same thing: a want. Anyway' ... impatiently ... 'you should remember that
Carol arrived after I did.'

'But you still knew she was coming, so you came as
well.'

'No. Oh, hell, we've been through all this before.'

But Zenith was not listening to him. 'If Dad has to
have Carol,' she said angrily, 'at least let him. Oh, I admit I don't like her, but if Dad——' Yet even as she
said it she remembered her father's gentle refusal of
Carol again, his delayed date for their wedding cere-
mony. Autumn taking its time with spring, she thought,
when autumn hasn't the time. Oh, it was all too confus-
ing.

'I'm going back,' she said abruptly. 'If you want to
come, come, if not——'

'I'll walk,' Steve answered.

Zenith got in the car and left.

She managed to get into the house unnoticed. She
went to the bathroom and removed what mud had not
been sponged away by Steve. By the time she had
finished and changed it was the hour to leave for dinner
at the canteen, for it had become an accepted thing now
for them to eat away from the house. Zenith wondered
if Dad had got over his disappointment on that account;
he had badly wanted that home touch, he had been so
obviously happy the night of Carol's arrival when
Helen had come to the rescue and served that splendid

meal, but if he was, then there was no sign. He tucked each girl's arm under his, and they strolled up to Jake's.

It was dance night again, and by this time the orchestra knew to soften the rhythm for the boss. Derek and Carol waltzed by, so close that Zenith wondered if her father had changed his mind over that wedding date, and whether he would announce it when the number was over and they all sat down again. She moved restlessly in Brent's arms, and he tightened the grasp he had on her. He had become the old Brent again, attentive, possessive, even devoted. After all, Zenith thought cruelly, she was the boss's daughter, so a safer bet for any ambitious young man than a boss's intended wife.

'Zenith, I hope you don't think I've been deserting you lately,' Brent said in Zenith's ear.

'Deserting me?'

'It's this wretched inundation business. It's certainly posed some problems.'

'Like you leaving?'

'Oh, dear me, no, I wouldn't think of deserting the sinking ship.'

'It's not sinking!' Zenith said sharply.

'You know what I mean, and by posing some problems I meant business problems. It's fallen to my lot to arrange for the ones who are considering leaving.'

'Are there many?'

'None,' Brent had to admit. 'Not even an enquiry. But naturally the families will have to begin to think about it, and as Savage is mainly family——'

'I can see my nursery school won't be needed,' Zenith regretted.

'That doesn't mean you'll go, too?' Brent asked anxiously.

'Never.'

'Then of course I won't, either.'

'Brent, why "of course"?'

A tender look from Brent that Zenith considered didn't suit him. '*You* must know that.'

'I don't, and certainly I haven't known it of late.'

'Then you *have* been aware of my—well—inattention.' Brent sounded quite gratified.

'No, but I have noticed your attention to Carol.'

'I can explain——' he began.

'Please don't, Brent. I know the explanation already. New girl. New face.'

'That was not my explanation,' Brent came in stiffly. 'I naturally felt as your father's second in command——'

'Helen is that,' she reminded him.

'Then right-hand man.'

'Steve Forbuck is that.' Zenith was repeating what Derek Smith had said of his new man on that first night.

'I naturally thought as the *accountant* I should do the right thing,' finished Brent.

Zenith did not hear him, she was on her own train of thoughts. She asked abruptly:

'How pretty a face, Brent?' Suddenly it seemed important to her to know how men, apart from Dad, saw Carol.

But Brent was on his guard now. He promptly drew any attention away from himself.

'For an answer you should ask our new man Mr Forbuck,' he advised. 'Ask why he's here.'

'To work, of course,' Zenith answered for Steve.

'After we'd stopped recruiting? Yes, that's true. As soon as Mr Smith became aware of the possible water

crisis, we stopped taking on any new people. Yet Forbuck still came.'

'He wouldn't be here without Dad's say-so, and he
must have the right credentials.'

'Also the right determination? But *what* determination? Would it be—*cherchez la femme*, do you think?'
Brent gave a sly look.

'You have a rotten accent, Brent,' Zenith said coldly.
She had had enough. She felt already on her own accord that Steve Forbuck had come after Carol, but she
still shrank from Brent's interpretation.

The music stopped and they sat down.

For the rest of the evening ... no, Dad made no new
announcement ... Zenith kept hearing Brent's '*cherchez la femme*, do you think?'

Looking at the pair concerned, at Steve and Carol,
certainly Zenith *had* to think. They were seated side
by side at the table for six, and every movement of
Carol's managed to include Steve Forbuck, and he did
not appear to object, indeed he was giving her long
enigmatical looks, no doubt, felt Zenith, *not* enigmatical
to Carol. She felt her nails pressing into her palms, and
flinched.

The morning of the Cooee Trial dawned as warmly
golden as ever, for in the Top End all days began this
way. Rain was an unusual event here, so much so that
some of the babies had never seen it, and would probably set up a cry when they did. And yet, Zenith mused,
Savage was now programmed, or so Dad and Steve
said, for a flood.

When Carol came out to join Zenith for the gala day
she was a vision in all white. 'All right,' she said crossly,

'just because I'm unfortunately situated in Savageville there's no reason for me to become one of the savages.'

'Meaning?'

'Take any meaning you wish,' Carol shrugged, but her glance up and down Zenith's jeans made her own meaning very apparent.

Zenith decided to let that pass, but not Carol's 'unfortunate situation.'

'Why don't you move out before the waters come?' she asked.

'*Are* they coming?'

'They might, so why don't you———'

'Why don't you mind your own business,' snapped Carol.

'I'm sorry, Carol, but if you hate it so much how will you abide it when you *have* to stay here?'

There was no pretence between them now; they simply disliked each other. 'I'll let you know,' promised Carol smoothly, '*in Sydney*.'

'*I* won't be in Sydney.'

'Afraid your father will make some move without you around to advise him?'

'I never advise Dad. Any decision he has made has been entirely on his own accord. On that trend, it might interest you to learn that I've even urged him to hurry things up.' A pause. 'With you.'

'It does interest me. Is it Brent or Steve you're nervous about in that urgency of yours?'

'I just want Dad's happiness, and if his happiness means you———'

'Oh, spare me the romantic frills. Are we going to this hick affair or not?'

'We're going,' Zenith almost gulped. 'You'll need

your helmet. Only the competitors who'll be out of Savage can discard them, the rest of us remain in the caution area, and Dad——' She stopped. Carol must have had her yellow helmet handy, for she slipped it on, slipped it provocatively, and, the same as before, the pale curls against the yellow metal did things helmets were not supposed to do. All at once more disconsolate than she had ever been, Zenith turned and went out to the jeep, and Carol followed her.

'Dad's there already,' she said tightly as they left. She felt near tears.

There were no tears in the town, though. The way it is with people who have little to amuse them, when something offers, however humble it is, it becomes important, and big, and great fun. All Savage was there, and the last thing you would have expected for these people was the prospect of a flood.

Jeep-loads of competitors were leaving for Wreck Mountain from where the entrants would shout their cooees, sing their cattle lullabies, do their bird imitations. To her horror Zenith saw Steve Forbuck among them. Suppose he——?

She moved across.

'Mr Forbuck——' she began.

He wheeled round and cocked one eyebrow at her.

'Good lord, here we are in the remote parallels, over five hundred kilometres to another living soul, and the lady addresses me as Mister! It even challenges Livingstone, I think.'

'Steve' ... she said it with difficulty and he grinned ... 'you're not in the contest, are you?'

'Certainly I am. I'm all for participation. Aren't you?'

'Well, yes, but——'

'Then why aren't you participating? I should think at least you would have entered the cattle singing. It would be good practice for later on.'

'Later on?'

'When you have your own family and need to sing them to sleep.'

'Very funny,' returned Zenith stiffly.

'Then if mirth is your speciality at least enter the jackass section.'

Zenith bit down on her lip to help her hold on to her temper. 'Please, I wanted to ask you something,' she appealed.

'Ask,' he shrugged.

'Is it the first section you're contesting?'

'Yes.'

'The cooee event?'

'Yes.'

'And you'll be—I mean——' she hesitated.

'Madam, the competition is for cooees. I think that's what's worrying you, isn't it?'

'Well, I hardly liked the idea of having my name bandied around,' she confessed.

'Even a name like Zenith?'

'Particularly a name like mine. If I were Jean, Joan, I could be someone else, but Zenith——'

'The greatest of heights and you object!'

'Only to "Zenith!" shouted from Wreck Mountain.'

'Then you're misnamed,' he sighed.

'All the same, you won't——'

'I'm an entrant and I would be eliminated at once.'

'Then thank you.'

'No, thank the rules of the contest—and thank your lack of imagination.'

'I will.' Zenith turned away.

She did not hear the cooee contest, she busied herself in the refreshment section shutting her ears to the calls, quite an easy accomplishment in the babble. She heard later that one of the miners had won, his working mate carrying off the other two sections. The cattle singing had been so good several of the mothers had reported their babies as falling off to sleep at once.

Only the beer drinking remained, and not wishing to watch that, Zenith slipped away from the scene and began walking back to the boss's house.

Like all the Inside nights, for it was night now, it was a glorious evening, big blobs of stars, a melon of a moon, a sky that could have been a theatre backdrop. All at once Zenith heard steps behind her, steps reaching her. She did not have to peer in the melon moonlight, she could see quite plainly. Steve Forbuck must have followed her.

'Not entering the final contest?' she asked coldly.

'Doesn't look like it, does it?' he returned cheerfully.

'I thought you might have liked to have won one at least.'

'Oh, I haven't lost,' he assured her. 'Far from it.'

'How do you mean?'

'If I thought you could understand I'd tell you.'

'If you mean Carol——'

'I told you that you wouldn't understand. But leave all that now, just come with me.'

'Come where?' she asked.

'Down the slope. Don't be alarmed, you're safe.' She sensed rather than saw his teasing grin, for the moon temporarily had gone behind a cloud.

He pulled her with him, but before she could pull back he stopped abruptly, stopping her with him. He knelt down, making her kneel as well. She made a small sound of protest, went to withdraw, then gasped as his hand grabbed hers and pushed it into something cool and wet.

It was water.

CHAPTER SIX

'WATER!'

Zenith said it breathlessly, incredulously. There was no water in Savage, not even at the bottom of the cuts. Yet here ... and she tried it a second time ... was water springing from the ground, only a small impulse as yet, but a continual one; she could feel the gentle but determined escape of it. The quiet bubble kept up its trickle, and she whispered to Steve: 'Water ... but it can't be!'

'It is, though, and it's come just as I said it would—from a break in the river that flows underneath.'

'A river underneath! What are you talking about?'

'A subterranean river. In old terrain like this is upside-down rivers are not unique. It's happened in other aged countries as well.'

'You mean reversal?'

'Yes. The dry earth on top, the river down below. Only sometimes, when fed from another impetus, the river can outgrow itself and break its subterranean bank. This one has. The impetus here would come from the receding inundation that surrounded Big Billy. The extra moisture passed on has proved just too much, and this has happened.' He nodded to the new spring.

It was all too much for Zenith, too. She remained

kneeling where he had put her and begged: 'Will you tell me more, please, Steve?'

She saw his face in the melon moonlight and it was a serious face. He tested the water again, then told her.

'I took this subject at university.'

'Subject?' she queried.

'Hydrography, which is the investigation of water. I did pretty well—so well indeed that when your father appealed to the powers-that-be for someone who knew what they were talking about and the powers recommended me, I had no false modesty about accepting the post.'

'Dad requested that?'

'Derek Smith is a wise ore man. He knew that a change was beginning in his terrain—a wetness here, a dampness there, less parching than the year before. So he offered me the job, and I came.'

'Brent Davids gave a different reason,' Zenith proffered. 'His reason for your coming was—*cherchez la femme.*'

'Yes, Brent would say that ... little realising he was very near right.'

'Very near right?'

'The job was a challenge ... but so was something else.'

'I think you mean some*one* else.'

'Look, you asked me to tell you about this.' He nodded to the spring.

'Yes, I did. I'm sorry. Please go on.'

'That day at Wreck Mountain I was water-hunting, not following you. I'd previously decided that there were three points where the subterranean bank could break, out there, in here, and——'

'And?'

'Later,' he dismissed. 'I was right at Wreck—you know that now from the sponging I gave you. Now I'm proved right here.'

There was silence for a moment, Zenith still incredulous.

'What will happen?' she asked at last.

'Going on the initial two evidences only a very gradual, innocuous inundation. But it's the third breakaway that really concerns me.'

'You mean you've already found a third?'

'Yes. Small yet, but with more potential. Until I know definitely from its progress everything must be kept low key. A stampede out of Savage is the last thing we need.'

'We haven't any horses.' Zenith tried to be facetious.

'More pertinent,' he broke in, 'we have only one plane.'

She looked at him again in the melon moonlight. 'You really are serious, aren't you?'

'Yes.'

'Then I'm sorry, but I can't be serious as well, in fact I can't even believe you.'

'Nor your father?'

'I'm sure Dad's not that concerned.'

'Then think again, Miss Smith ... but don't take too long over your thinking.'

'Will there be time,' she asked flippantly, 'for me to get home before I have to swim?'

'You know I mean no such thing, you know I'm really referring to Savage's serious acceptance of a fact, followed, if the event happens, by a systematic evacuation.'

'My, such big words for a water man!' she baited. 'Anyway, Brent Davids is looking after all that.'

'Only on paper so far, and not too attentively. Zenith, listen to me: *things have to begin.*'

'But you said gradual, innocuous inundation.'

'From these two instances, yes, but what about my third? It's the third that's worrying me, you see. Something has to be started, but without panic. Panic is the last thing we can afford. That's why so far there's only been understatement even to your father ... but not now to you.'

'I'm honoured,' she said drily.

'No, you are *told*,' Steve said. 'How can I convince you that we must make haste but for our own sakes make it slowly?'

'You can't,' she answered, 'and now that I know it's still safe to move, I'll go home.'

There was a sharp silence, only the steady trickle of water breaking it, then:

'Quite safe from that,' Steve agreed thickly, 'but safe from—this?'

His sudden quick lunge forward took Zenith completely by surprise, one moment she was kneeling beside him, the next moment she was enclosed helplessly in strong arms, iron-hard arms, and the tight grasp was tightening, it was imprisoning her so entirely that she felt herself losing her kneeling balance and sinking down to the ground. She sensed more than saw that he was descending with her.

Now his arms had left her and instead he was taking her face in his hands and kissing her. Zenith could have moved away, for no longer was she imprisoned, and his caress was just that, just a brush of his lips, yet she did not move, *she could not*. She felt him running his fingertips through her hair, then the fingers explored her eyelids, ears, nape of her neck, hollow of her throat. Close by she could hear the water in soft explosion, she could feel the cool dampness of the earth under her.

'It's another world.' She heard him as if a long way off. 'It's the world I've been exploring these last few weeks, a world as old as creation itself. It's a primal world, a Dreamtime world, it's not Now, nor even Yesterday, it's millions of years ago, and you, woman, are making a tribal man of me.'

His lips came down on hers, and it was not a caress, not a brush this time, it was a kiss. Suddenly as primitive as he was, Zenith kissed him back. For a few seconds that seemed to go into eternity they stopped entwined in each other's arms, then, with a little gasp, Zenith broke loose.

'Are you a hypnotist or something?' she gasped.

'Something.' He had got up and was extending a hand, which she ignored, for her to get up as well.

'My apologies.' His voice was dry. 'Can you swim back?'

She did not answer him, she was running up the slope to escape him, and it was only when she had reached the boss's house that she realised he had not come after her. She stood on the verandah a moment, catching her breath, touching, though unaware of it, her neck and throat where his fingers had touched.

Through the darkness she heard steps from the direction of the community hall, and she knew it would be her father and Carol returning from the final event.

She ran down the hall and had her light out before they came in.

'Zennie must have been tired,' she heard Dad say sympathetically.

'I don't wonder.' Carol's voice hardly hid a petulance.

At once their lights were out as well. It was always like this, Zenith frowned in the darkness; it wasn't right, even for spring and autumn lovers, not to wait up to talk, not to——

In the room's deep shadows suddenly Zenith's cheeks were burning. She was remembering a tribal man and a primitive woman tonight. What can he be thinking of me? She touched her burning cheeks again.

But it appeared he was thinking of himself as well. In the morning her father handed Zenith an envelope.

'Letter under the door for you, Zennie.' He was uninterested, but Carol, who had come out in a stunning negligee, was looking at the message curiously.

Aware of her intrigue, Zenith took the letter inside and opened it.

'Having changed our time slot last night surely we should now delve deeper. Woman, I shall meet you after my shift.'

He did not sign it, not even initial it. He wouldn't, Zenith thought.

She wouldn't meet him, of course, and she wouldn't delve ... whatever that meant.

She was still telling herself this when Steve Forbuck's jeep pulled up at the door, she was still insisting it as she obeyed his quick flip of the horn and went out.

She was saying it foolishly as he released the brake and as he plunged the rough little four-wheeled drive into a track she had never noticed before, merely two thin lines of imprints that could have been a whim of the wind, but evidently were not, for Steve Forbuck knew where he was going . . . and went.

'You've been here before,' Zenith said a little breath-lessly, breathless from the bumps, for the track was not a formed one, and went willy-nilly over roots, rock out-crops, fallen logs.

'Yes, I've been looking around,' he told her.

'For water?'

'I found that; it's that third piece of evidence I told you about. But I also found people—a tribe of people. Anthropology was another of my varsity subjects, an-other love.'

'You have a variety of loves,' she commented.

'Yet actually only one.' He took his eyes off the track for a moment to look at Zenith. 'I call the others loves, too, but there's really just one.'

'She's the one you came for.'

'No, she is not.'

She sighed. 'I don't understand you.'

'That's all right, we didn't come for understanding, not this time, we came to delve deeper.'

'So your note said, but meaning——?'

'Meaning we were primitives last night, so now we go on from there.'

'Oh, no, we don't.'

'You misunderstand me,' he corrected. 'We go on from there by meeting our fellow primitives. In short there's a tribe out here I'm checking. Do you know them?'

'I've heard of them,' said Zenith, 'and Dad knew them once. It was while I was at school. Dad tried to keep them in Savage for their own good, better nutri-tion and all that, and some of them did stay a while, but then they left.'

'Yes, they would do that.'

'He treated them very well,' she assured him.

'I'm sure he did.' Steve was concentrating on his driving, for he was manoeuvring his way now between two giant anthills.

'This camp I'm taking you to is entirely myall,' he told her. 'Do you know what that means?'

'True aboriginal,' she nodded, 'nothing added.'

'As they were in the beginning,' he agreed. 'Possibly,' he went on, 'we won't see any at all, not at this time of day. The men will be out hunting and the women tagging along to help. Or it might even be a honey search, where the man focuses the bee and follows him while his woman calls out the lay of the land.' He added meaningly : 'Or else.'

'That's not fair,' protested Zenith, 'it's harder to run and call out than just run after a bee.'

'You try it,' he challenged. 'But don't complain when you get what a lot of them get if the man loses the bee by tumbling over.'

'No honey?'

He turned round from the wheel again and eyed her briefly. 'You're kidding,' he said, and grinned. 'No, they get a wallop, and full strength I say to the walloping hand.'

'Yes, you would say,' Zenith shot back at him.

'*Yicki,*' he advised suddenly, then he explained, '*Yicki* is what you should have shouted just now when I nearly collided with that boulder.'

'*Yicki?*' she queried.

'Beware. Look out.'

'Then you already know some of the language.'

'There are a few general words that every tribe uses; also I picked up some other words when I came out on my water investigations. Not much, but all in all it helps.'

'The water,' she reminded him.

'I'm going to show it to you now. But before that——'

'Yes?'

He had pulled up the jeep, and he looked hard at her. Before she could 'misunderstand' again he asked: 'Are you a believer, or disbeliever, in lore, Zenith?'

'Aboriginal lore?'

'Yes.'

'I've never considered it, but I think I'd believe. Why?'

'A story I was told by the tribe's Pouri Pouri man. That's Witch Doctor to you, and among the myalls, until they go into the missions, the belief in him remains.'

'Please go on.'

'Mostly the Pouri Pouri cures consist of wax from wild bees buried for weeks in an anthill, or a snake's nest—other astonishing things.

'Then of course there's the pointing of the bone, which also requires the Pouri Pouri man's advice. He's called in, but he can't do much. The unfortunate victim's imagination sees to that.'

'He dies?' queried Zenith.

'Yes. You see, the victim won't let himself sleep in case the Debil-Debil gets him. He won't eat in case of poison. And so he fades out. But I wasn't listening to that particularly, rather was I interested in the Pouri Pouri's story of the water.

'Years ago there was much water here, so my friendly M.D. said.'

'Be serious!' she begged.

'Believe me, I am.' He gave her a long look. 'Beside the water lived a big snake, and the snake would cool himself from the heat by resting in the water. Then a big bird ... everything, you'll note, is big here ... swooped down over the snake, but the wise snake at once went underground, shrewdly taking the water with him.'

'So from that fairytale you build up another reason for our approaching waters.' Zenith gave a laugh.

'Perhaps I do, perhaps I don't, but it's an old, strange country, so who can say?'

He climbed out of the jeep and nodded for Zenith to follow him. She knew he was about to show her his third evidence, and she came behind him sceptically, until——

They found it together under a clump of cabbage palm: a deep ... *very deep* ... stream.

'It can't be,' Zenith protested. She walked up and down the bank. 'Was it like this before?'

'It wasn't here before. I really mean it wasn't here on my first visit.'

'Then?'

'But there was a certain sponginess that alerted me, brought me back again to re-check.'

'Yes?'

'I found a trickle. The next time I found a stream. Now there's this. Zenith, in several days the thing has risen noticeably.'

They stared at the busy ripple, then they looked at each other.

'So,' surrendered Zenith, 'it's not your imagination.'

'No.'

4 FREE Harlequin Romances

Take these  best-selling Harlequin Romance stories FREE

... ◄ EXCITING DETAILS INSIDE

BUSINESS REPLY MAIL —

No postage stamp necessary if mailed in the United States.

Postage will be paid by

Harlequin Reader Service
901 Fuhrmann Blvd.,
Buffalo, N.Y.
14203

FIRST CLASS
PERMIT No. 8907
Buffalo, N.Y.

'So,' she went on, 'we have to begin.'

'Yes,' he agreed, 'we begin. But first I want to see the men. When the waters spread there has to be some system. For instance the women, the piccaninnies and the old men will all have to be brought in.'

'To Savage?'

'Where else? I want you to wait here, Zenith. Forget the things that I said about going on from last night——'

'I forgot them last night,' she assured him.

'And keep quiet.' He ignored her interruption. 'Don't move around, they mightn't like it.'

'They?' she asked.

'Our fellow primitives.' He gave a maddening grin. But at once he was serious again. 'Just stay here,' he said.

'Would they know if I didn't?'

'Certainly. I can't take you with me because you wouldn't be accepted yet.'

Zenith nodded. At least she knew that law, everyone out here knew it. A man had to present himself first, then, if they agreed, he could bring in a woman. She watched Steve push through the undergrowth, disappear under the cabbage palms, then she turned to the stream again. She looked at it for quite a while, busy, bubbling, not even time for gnats. She threw in a few leaves, followed their passage, then she decided to return to the jeep.

She sat and waited in the jeep, aware, the way one is aware, that she was being watched by someone, but no matter how hard she looked, she could not see by whom. She wondered how these women would react if what Steve proposed to do eventuated. She could not see them in Savage, not the bigger, busier Savage that it was now. Dad had told her that even in the early days they had found it too large to comprehend, and had left, so what would they think this time? She also could not see Carol there with them ... certainly not Carol.

Presently Steve came out of the bushes again, and gave her a rueful look.

'Big trouble,' he said.

He started the jeep, and as they retraced their way he told her.

'There's been a tribal shindy, a very serious one.'

'Anyone hurt?'

'Only a brave from a neighbouring attacking tribe. These Bildies ... that was the name ... attacked our braves here, and there was a skirmish and an accidental death.'

'Oh, dear!' sighed Zenith.

'That's not the worry, that killing was legitimate and accepted by all, all's fair in love and war and all that. No, Zenith, the offence was Avua breaking the rule.'

'Avua?' she queried.

'One of the home warriors.'

'The rule?' she asked.

'A halt on both sides for a night's wailing over the body. It's always been done, but Avua——'

'But Avua didn't?'

'No. Auva crept out under cover of the mourning and the wailing and has not been seen since. The opposing tribe are scandalised, but their shock is nothing to the home tribe's deep disgrace.'

'Who told you all this?' asked Zenith.

'The old men. The young ones have gone after Avua, they've gone far, the old men say, for Avua is a quick mover. But' ... a hunch of Steve's shoulders ... 'by the look of our third piece of evidence just now, our trickle turned stream, I'll be surprised if either Avua or his pursuers will be seen for many a day.'

'They'll be cut off?'

'No doubt about it. And without her man to tell her what to do there's not one lubra who'll move from here. Unlike our lot, the women obey.' He gave Zenith a sidelong look.

'I think you may be proved wrong,' Zenith said coldly. 'I believe these women will show themselves as cool-headed and as liberated as we are. When the moment comes——'

'When it comes they'll stand and wait for the men's say-so. Women. Never underestimate their pestilence.'

'Even when they obey?' asked Zenith slyly.

'Their obedience is only a cover, their pestilence is themselves. They start everything. One even started this trouble we face now. It's a woman behind Avua's disappearance, have no doubt about that.'

'I would have a doubt. Avua may have grown sick of wailing.'

'More like it he grew sick for his Ludy's arms.'

'Ludy?' she questioned.

'Now being guarded by several of the women in case she, too, flies off.'

'After Avua?'

'Yes.'

'If I were a guard,' Zenith said, 'I'd let her go.'

Another quick glance from Steve, even though the going was rough and needed all his attention. 'I never put you down as a romanticist,' he remarked, 'as a primitive, decidedly, but as a—— Hi, stop that!' For

Zenith had raised her hand angrily at him.

'You're hateful!' she flung.

'But right?'

'It was just for a moment last night.'

'You mean a moon and all that?'

'Please take me back,' she said angrily.

He did so in silence for a while, then he said: 'We couldn't let Ludy go, you know. She'll have to be brought in. You see, there's going to be a baby, and a baby in a flood——'

'A baby!'

'It does happen when you're young and in love. Now why are you laughing?'

'No reason really, except I was suddenly thinking of Carol.'

'Carol?' he queried.

'How will Carol take to an obstetric ward in the rec room?' Zenith giggled again.

He kept driving, but as they bounced back to Savage Zenith could see that he was beginning to grin as well.

In a time of seriousness, as they now had before them, Zenith was glad there was a moment, however brief, for mirth.

CHAPTER SEVEN

As soon as they got back into the town Steve sought out Derek Smith. The last Zenith saw of him was closing Dad's office door, closing it firmly. The two men were cloistered for hours, and Zenith knew there would be no canteen dinner that night.

'Where is everybody?' Carol asked fretfully. As usual she had changed ... she always dressed up for the evening meal ... and she looked down on her stunning blue sheath with disgust.

'Savage is no misnomer,' she muttered, 'the place is little short of barbaric!'

Zenith forbore to remind her of the obvious remedy, that of going back to civilisation, for she knew that at once Carol would change her tune.

'I'll go when I'm ready,' she had said last time. 'Just keep out of this, Zenith.'

After that Zenith had only exchanged everyday commonplaces with Carol, got no deeper, but in all fairness she felt that the boss's intended wife should be as informed as the boss's daughter on the latest development. Painstakingly then she told Carol, but too painstakingly it seemed, for in the end it came out in unintelligible mumbo-jumbo ... Carol called it gobbledygook ... with hydrology mixed hopelessly up with great snakes that go underground and take rivers with them.

'What on earth are you babbling about?' Carol demanded. 'Really, Zenith, you must have caught something from your pre-schoolers, some infantile complaint.'

'It's what Dad has been saying.' Zenith tried again. 'The inundation of water from Big Billy.'

'Oh, that!'

'Yes, that. But this time it's serious, Carol. You see——'

Zenith began it all again, this time leaving out the legend, leaving in only the facts as provided by Steve Forbuck.

'So you've been seeing Steve?' Carol interrupted.

'I'm speaking of what Mr Forbuck had to report, not the man himself.'—'Mr Forbuck!' Steve had marvelled that day of the cooee contest, 'here we are five hundred kilometres to a living soul and Mr Forbuck! It even challenges Livingstone, I think.'

'Perhaps not the man himself but spoken by the man himself,' Carol smiled thinly.

'He said——' Zenith, firming her lips, proceeded to tell Carol.

'That silly old rumour again,' Carol scoffed. 'I've never heard anything so absurd in all my life. What's Steve trying to do? Clear us all out? Of course there couldn't be any such thing as a flood. You have only to look outside.' She waved a lovely white arm.

Zenith followed the direction of her wave, and felt almost like agreeing with her. The sky was banner blue today, the earth beneath its inverted bowl lay red, in places cracked, and dry, dry, dry.

However, facts remained, and she gave Carol these facts.

'I don't believe it,' Carol said, 'just as I don't believe Steve Forbuck. After all' ... a secret look ... '*I* should know. We were at the same project together before this one—I rather think you've gathered that.'

Zenith admitted, 'Yes, I had gathered it.'

'He didn't stay long ... he hasn't stayed long anywhere ... but he stayed long enough at Silverstream Hydro for me to find out he was a liar.'

'I don't want to hear it.' (Zenith did, though.) 'I want you to realise our present position.'

Carol ignored her.

'He always made a big thing of not wanting women around ... even me ... but you could see very clearly that he was still looking for someone.'

'At a hydro?'

'Also at the other projects he had been in before Silverstream,' hinted Carol. 'There were——'

'A string,' nodded Zenith. 'He told me.'

'As well as telling you this latest gobbledygook.'

'It isn't!' Zenith insisted.

'Well, you might believe it ... and *him*, but I wouldn't. But seeing you're believing, I'll give you a warning: Steve Forbuck is after something ... some*one* ... and all his talk of not liking women is as sound as his silly inundation theory. The man is looking for a certain female. It can't be for looks, or it would have been me,' Carol said with a shrug. 'It could be for gain, which could include you, but not to all that extent now that I've come on the scene. But there *is* someone somewhere, have no two thoughts about that ... and now at last those two are coming out of hiding.'

Derek and Steve were indeed emerging, but it was not to be for long. Without waiting to explain, or apologise, Derek went past Carol and Zenith who had climbed up to the huddle of offices to wait for the men, and, summoning Brent Davids, instructed the accountant to bring all the branch executives to the head office at once. Emergency meeting, Zenith heard.

Carol heard it, too, and snorted. Nonetheless all the executives arrived, and once more the door was firmly shut.

Zenith suggested a cup of coffee in the canteen, but Carol was quite furious by now.

'All this cloak and dagger stuff, what do they think they're about?'

'They may be ages. We'd better eat something, Carol.'

Carol's bottom lip was out. Apart from Derek, Steve, Brent and a few ... very few ... unattached clerical side bachelors, she had no interest in the canteen. Anyone worth considering, her look said clearly, was behind that closed door.

But at last Zenith did persuade her, and the two of them crossed to Jake's.

At once Carol gave a hunch of disgust, and looking into the room Zenith saw that the hunch was because of Helen. It had to be Helen. There was no one else present.

'That woman——' Carol muttered.

'She has more right to be here than us, really, she comes under the single category, and because of that has sleeping digs but no kitchen.'

'Yes, you've said all that before, but why is she always around? Come to think of it, why is she here at Savage at all?'

'To earn her living, I suppose,' supplied Zenith. It had never occurred to her to question Helen why she should choose to work in such a remote place as here.

'Because she hasn't been successful in the marriage race,' went on Carol, 'we're inflicted with her.'

'It's not an infliction, it's an honour,' retorted Zenith. 'I love Helen. Also I haven't been matrimonially successful myself as yet.' Zenith could have added: 'Actually you haven't yourself.'

Carol was not listening to her, she was asking Jake what he had to offer at this hour, and putting no charm in her question. Carol never wasted herself on anyone she did not need to impress.

Knowing she was wrong there, knowing, from Dad, that an army marches on its stomach, Zenith stepped forward and coaxed some toasted sandwiches out of Jake. While Carol chose a seat ... away from Helen ... she chatted with Jake, and naturally the conversation came round to the emergency meeting.

'Hush-hush in the exec room,' said Jake, putting sandwiches under the griller.

'Yes, Jake.'

'Reckon we all know what it's about, though. So the inundation is to be a fact of life, Zennie.'

'So they say.'

'I'll be sorry if I have to go,' he went on. 'I've liked this outfit. But I'll find another—always have.'

'*You* won't be going, Jake, we couldn't do without you.'

'Reckon you'll have to. I'm a *big* meat and potatoes

man, not a little family retainer. And I reckon after the workers go it will be a *very* little family, little enough for you to fend for yourselves.'

'What was the fellow saying?' Carol asked when Zenith took along the tray.

'He was telling me that very shortly we'll be getting our own meals,' Zenith said, and had the satisfaction of seeing Carol look far from pleased. She checked her glee at Carol's dismay, though, with the mental reminder that when it came to cooking she was no great shakes herself.

She put down the coffee and sandwiches, then, ignoring Carol and her undoubted objections, she went across to Helen and asked her to join them. After all, the three of them could not sit apart in a big hall like this.

Carol, moody at first, must have had a change of mind.

'An insidious position, isn't it?' she actually smiled to Helen.

'Unfortunate,' permitted Helen.

'... You've been here since Savage's inception,' Carol went on smoothly, 'or so Derek tells me.'

'Yes, that's true.'

'Then you can't say you've been tossed from pillar to post.'

'No, Miss Quinn, I can't.'

'Not like our new man Steve Forbuck, for instance. He has a long string of previous assignments. Probably unsuitable at each, I would think.'

'No, I wouldn't think that.'

'But you still wouldn't know, would you?'

'Only what Mr Smith tells me.'

'Which would not be what *Derek* tells me,' said Carol, suddenly sick of the polite conversation. 'Aren't those men ever coming out of that meeting? I'm fed up with this preposterous delay. I'm going back to the house to bed.' She looked at Zenith. 'You can tell your father that.'

Zenith, longing to stop up, hear the news, learn the findings, even remain in the canteen to apologise to Helen, got up as well. She knew the track down to the house by heart. Carol didn't. She didn't like the girl, she knew she never would, but she did not want the future Mrs Derek Smith to fall and break her leg.

Back in the house Carol did as she said she would, she went straight to bed.

Zenith sat up for over an hour, then she, too, went to her room. She read ... and never absorbed one word ... for another hour.

But Dad did not return all that night. Afterwards Zenith learned that the meeting went well into the morning, but after her initial listening she lost consciousness of time and the fact that her father still was not home, and she slept.

When she awoke everything at first seemed the same ... Carol's door closed as it always was ... Dad's room empty but the bed made, for he was an early riser and he left things like that, neat, shipshape.

But up in the town a siren was shrilling, an *alarm* siren, and when Zenith went out on the verandah to see why she glimpsed something that looked like a sign tacked to the executive door, she saw people already flocking to read it.

Zenith raced up in her short housegown and craned her neck, too.

An important public meeting, the handwritten notice announced, within the hour. Everyone to attend.

Everyone.

Quite unconscious of her skimpy attire, for all the wives were skimpy-clad, too, Zenith lingered with the Savages, wondering with them, agreeing with them, hoping with them, until she remembered the star guest —Carol. It was getting towards the time when Carol usually stirred from her slumber. She had better get back and break the news.

Or had she better do that? Would it be more in keeping to leave it to Derek? Yet Dad had enough on his plate, too much really. What to do?

As usual Zenith searched out Helen.

Helen was fully dressed. Like Dad, she was an early riser. Derek often had reported that he had seen Helen walking round the Cut in the early hours. He had said it with approval, obviously it had pleased him that his secretary would find enough interest in the place to take a stroll around it on her own accord. And yet ... and yet he had chosen *Carol*, who had never put one foot forward in Savage apart from attending the canteen.

'Helen, it looks grim, doesn't it?' Zenith asked when she reached the older woman.

'It's serious, yes, but not grim, not yet.'

'Serious enough to tell Carol?'

Helen considered, taking off her glasses as she always did when she thought, putting them back again when she had come to a decision.

As she watched her Zenith gave a little involuntary start. For the first time since she had known Helen she was oddly aware of a recognition. A recognition of what, she could not have said, she just felt ... but felt strongly ... she had seen eyes like Helén's hazelnut eyes before. Not the colour, but the setting, the direct look.

'Have I a smudge on my nose?' Helen laughed.

'No—no, of course not. I'm very sorry. Do I tell her or not, Helen? Do I leave it to Steve?'

'I think our men won't be having any time for disclosures, Zenith, other than public disclosures. Yes, tell her, then bring her up here for the meeting.'

'Yes, Helen.'

Zenith went back down the slope.

Carol was on the verandah, and cross as usual. Whenever things did not go as she pleased she changed into the other sullen Carol, particularly if there was no one who mattered to observe the change. Zenith did not matter, so Carol all but attacked her.

'What the heck is going on?' she demanded.

'The balloon's gone up, Carol.'

'Speak properly!' snapped Carol.

'Well, I think ... we all think ... things have come to a head. There's to be a public meeting within the hour.'

'Concerning what?'

'The floodwaters.'

'Oh, that again!'

'We believe so. Carol, it's dead serious this time. Are you coming or not?'

Carol considered a moment, looked Zenith up and down, then directed: 'I won't be long.' She went inside and presently returned in a gown that would have melted the ice on Mount Everest, Zenith thought. She seemed to be enjoying it all, no doubt anticipating the looks she would get up at the meeting. She had a lot to learn, Zenith knew. Men faced with what these men faced wouldn't be aware if a woman wore a chaff bag.

This is their future. This is survival, life itself.

'Don't run,' Carol complained, 'I'm still in my mules.'

By the time they reached the notice board the entire town had gathered at the bottom of the shallow steps leading to the executive offices. There was a small verandah outside the offices, and on the verandah stood a group of Savage representatives. Zenith noticed the paymaster, the bio-chemist, the analyst, the top man of each of the working gangs.

The door opened and Brent Davids joined the group. Then Steve Forbuck came out. Last of all Derek Smith. Zenith thought she had never seen her father look more weary.

He came to the edge of the steps and looked down on the assembly.

'There is not one of you here who hasn't been conscious of the evacuation rumours that have been going the Savage rounds in the last few weeks. In the beginning that's what they were: rumours. Then evidence began to build up ... I'll leave it to our hydro specialist to tell you the details ... until last night I, and the men who run this outfit, faced a truth. The truth is this: Savage faces almost certain inundation. There is no physical peril, you'll all be out by that, and even if some of you stay, as I shall myself, you would not be in actual danger, for the storage capacity of the town's open cuts and the safer height of our summit, which happens to be right here, would prevent that. In fact if the worst did happen, then you could wipe out all this continent.' A shrug. 'All the world.

'But you won't be facing disaster, you'll be leaving. There'll only be room for a skeleton staff, a few caretakers, you could almost say, minding the place until

Savage can function again. For it will function, I promise you that, and when it does I want you all back again, because I value my men.' Derek Smith paused, then set his gaze on the women. 'And I value my men's mates.'

Beside Zenith, Carol moved restlessly. She's bored, Zenith knew. But a woman in the next row began to cry quietly, and the little soft sound touched gently on Zenith's sore heart.

She had tears in her own eyes when one of the men began to cheer. They all took it up, and, stepping forward again, Derek Smith put up his hand. He looked younger once more, Zenith noted.

'Thank you,' he said, obviously touched. 'Thank you. Now over to Steve Forbuck.'

Steve stepped forward and the crowd pushed in.

It was a difficult report that Steve had to make. He had to tell these men why they were being paid off, why they had to leave, why there was a grave urgency when everything looked so innocuous. He had to make it simple, convincing, believable, most of all the only possible thing to do. He could have skirted round the reasons, but evidently he and Derek had discussed that and decided to disclose every detail, both scientific and technical, and to present it to the workers in as honest, simple and direct manner as possible.

From his opening words it was obvious he was the right man for the job. Even Zenith's 'muscle boys', those yellow ants who toiled at the sides and the base of the cuts, workers unashamedly here only for the big wages, obviously followed and applauded every word. Steve even brought in the old aboriginal legend, and there was not one laugh, only a thoughtful nodding of helmeted heads.

'A very successful performance,' Carol said sarcastically. 'He'll take at least three curtains, don't you think?'

Zenith did not answer, for if she was hearing she was not heeding. Instead she was looking at Helen. Helen was standing in front of her, she could see her in profile, and there was a tenseness in the woman she had never known before. Helen was always such a calm person, such an undisturbed person. Now, if not perhaps disturbed, she was certainly very, *very* alert. Her mouth, a rather generous and sweet mouth, had its lips a little apart, her eyes were wide and intent. Intent on —Steve. Yes, there was no denying that. Helen was looking at Steve with—why, it was longing. Zenith turned her own glance sensitively away, ashamed at her discovery. Helen was old enough to be Steve Forbuck's mother, how could she have read longing in her?

Yet she was not the only one. Still at Zenith's side, Carol said silkily:' Love's young dream, would you say ... except one of them isn't young, is she?'

'I don't know what you're talking about,' said Zenith coldly.

'You know all right. I'd watch that young man if he were my young man.'

Zenith snapped, 'You sicken me, Carol!'

'But he obviously doesn't sicken her.' A soft little laugh.

Zenith pushed away from her, she went right to the back of the crowd. Here she could hear Steve still talking, still holding everyone as though he had them in the hollow of his hand.

But she could also still see Helen. Helen hanging on Steve's every word.

CHAPTER EIGHT

As early as the next morning the evacuation began. Derek Smith, once he had made the decision, would have liked to have started immediately, but the process had to be done systematically, and though everyone had known all about it for some time, no serious preparation had been made.

'It's not my fault,' Brent Davids complained to anyone who would listen, 'I called for applicants to leave, but no one came forward and gave their name.'

'No one is blaming you.' Zenith, who had been sent to Brent's office with a first list, *had* to listen. 'You can't force people ... well, you couldn't then. Now there's no choice. Here are the names Dad had put down for the first load.'

'Any news of any contributing plane yet?' Brent asked, scanning the list.

'Dad is on to it now. It's going to be hard, though, we're so far out for a small plane to come to our assistance, and we haven't the room for a proper sized aircraft to put down.'

'And no formed road for surface exit,' Brent muttered. 'What a country!'

'You sound just like Carol,' Zenith commented.

'How?'

'She's always saying we're primitive.'

Brent looked up, moistened his rather full mouth, looked down again. But he said nothing.

Zenith went out again to do what her father had asked her, and that was help the women. Not that there was much to help with. Nothing save personal belongings could be taken out, the plane would be over-encumbered as it was with human cargo.

The women had been told this, but Zenith still did not find her job easy. There was not one pre-fab door she knocked on that did not open up to some red-eyed wife, reluctant to leave some small domestic trifle (but still surplus cargo) she had come to treasure and now had to discard.

'But this was my very first wedding gift,' Jenny All-sopp cried when Zenith gently disengaged her from a toaster. Young Jenny and her husband had come here as newly-marrieds. 'Look.' Jenny indicated a strange object tacked to the wall of her kitchen. Zenith went across and examined the black disc.

'Our first toast. Bill nailed it there for posterity.' Jenny added unnecessarily: 'I burned it.'

'It can still be for posterity,' said Zenith, a little prickle-eyed herself.

'You mean I can take the toaster?'

'No.'

'Then the toast?'

'Jenny, no. When I said for posterity I meant that you and Bill will be back here to make—burn—more toast.' But Zenith said it unconvinced, and she knew that Jenny was not convinced, either.

She averted her eyes every time she passed the kindergarten. When next would she arrange a row of sleeping mats and put a line of different-hued small heads down to rest?

Naturally women and children were to be evacuated first, but ... naturally again ... most of the women would not leave without their husbands. This meant more lists, more delay.

'No hassle,' Steve Forbuck advised ... he had come into the office as Zenith was wrestling with the names ... 'it won't be that quick.'

'The water?'

'Yes.'

'How quick?' Zenith asked.

'More insidious than quick. Not here a moment ago, but here now.'

'That *is* quick!' she said anxiously.

'Not the way you are thinking, for that's not the way it will come. There'll be no roaring torrent, no rushing flood, nothing like that. It will simply creep in, spread, and you'll soon be wondering what it was like when it wasn't there.'

'You mean the sea around us?'

'Yes.' A pause. 'Are you down on the list?'

'Of course not.'

'No "of course" about it, but I won't press the matter. Not yet. It looks as though we have our hands full for the next few days.'

'Only a few days? I thought it would take a week.'

'We've had good news. An aircraft has been directed to us—bigger than our own old faithful, yet still not too big to put down on our small strip. With two on the job instead of one——'

'Great,' nodded Zenith, 'I'll table another column of departees.'

For all their outward reluctance to leave, the majority of the women were plainly excited, some of them even ashamedly elated. When it came to a supermarket round the corner, movies, annual sales, the much larger pay envelope their husbands received and a near-free house offered little competition.

They were genuinely sad, though, as Zenith was sad. They knew, and Zenith knew, that in most cases they would never come back. They would either drift into city life, or find some other project. Savage would become a memory to them.

If Dad was finding it hard to lose his best hands, Zenith was finding it very hard to lose her children. She went out on the bus with each load of departees, and every time a pre-schooler went, she openly wept.

'The so-called flood will be here before it's scheduled if you keep going on like that,' Carol remarked once. Carol always seemed to be in the bus, too—why, Zenith did not know, she never said goodbye to anyone.

Carol looked very hard at the departing craft, though, very thoughtfully. She had never expressed any wish one way or other, not since the night in the canteen when she had suggested to Derek that they hurry along their wedding. But a lot of water had passed under the bridge since then. Water! Zenith grimaced. Why did she have to bring up the subject of water?

On the day that small Alexander left with his parents, his father the chief shot firer of the largest cut, his mother expecting Savage's first local-born baby, Zenith all but broke down.

'You were going to make history, Mary,' she reproached.

'I'll be back, Zen, and I'll promise you a local born

Savage even yet. Anyway, what's wrong with doing it yourself?'

'I'm not even married.' Zenith mopped her tears up and gave a watery smile.

'I don't believe that's the real reason at all, I believe young Trouble here has put you off babies for good.' Alexander's mother looked knowingly down on her son.

'Oh, no,' exaggerated Zenith, for Alexander *had* been trouble ... lovable trouble.

She peered closer at the three-year-old, and saw, in spite of luggage stipulations, that he carried something.

'I couldn't get it away from him,' Mary groaned.

'It can't go, Mary, Hugo's much too large, almost as large as another child.' Hugo was the kindergarten bear that Alexander had put in the bath. Unfortunately, under the present circumstances, the dunking had not shrunk him as one would have expected, indeed the bear had grown larger and floppier than ever.

'He can't go,' Zenith repeated weakly ... then let Hugo go, of course.

It was not until the Heron aircraft had merged into iron-ore distance that Zenith noticed that Steve Forbuck was also at the strip.

'What's going on?' he demanded. 'Why this preferential treatment for bears?'

'Alexander loved him,' she pleaded.

'Are you doing that with everybody, letting them take something they love.'

'Oh, no, Jenny couldn't take her toaster. Nor her burned toast.'

Steve looked at her with a show, either mock or genuine, of anxiety.

'Come in out of the sun,' he ordered.

In the tiny waiting hut, deserted now that the plane had left, he looked critically at her.

'It's tearing you to pieces, isn't it?' he quizzed.

'The work pace?'

'The abandonment of Savage, the departure of the families.'

'... Yes.' Zenith knew she had to admit it, for he had only to look at her to see for himself.

'Can't have you like that. There's too much ahead. Look, stop your farewells for the rest of the day. Give the job to Carol.'

'Carol comes out on every trip.' Zenith looked around half expecting to see Carol now, but the girl must have gone back in the bus.

'Yes,' said Steve drily, 'I've noticed that. Giving it a long, hard, speculative stare, would you say?' He looked quizzically at Zenith, but she had nothing to reply.

'Anyway, that was *your* last trip out for the day,' Steve went on. 'I'm going bush, and I need your help.'

'Help?' she queried.

'With the women, the lubras. We're going to where I took you before to see if any of the younger men have returned yet, and if not to drive home a few home truths to those who are in the camp.'

'The inundation, you mean?'

'Yes.'

'How can I help when I can't say one word and they can't say one word back to me?' she protested.

'Pantomime. Womanly intuition. One female to another. Just so long as they understand. If I were you I'd work on the piccaninnies—they're terribly proud of their babies. They would die on the spot to defend them. I've been noticing you, Zenith, and I reckon you'd do the same.'

'I have no babies,' she pointed out.

'Given time,' he said, and his eyes suddenly were holding hers, holding them in a way she could not have described. It was an effort to look away.

They did not drive back to Savage first, they plunged straight into the bush. Again Zenith wondered how the man beside her could find his way over the sketchy track.

When they reached their destination the first thing that Steve did was examine the stream. He let out a grunt as he parted some branches, and when Zenith came up behind him she gasped. It was not a stream any more, it was almost a creek.

'You see,' Steve said.

Zenith nodded, and stood obediently by the creek while he sought out some of the old men. Just as before Zenith was aware of eyes watching her, but eyes, she knew, that in terrain like this, in people like these people were, she would never see herself.

It was a long time before Steve returned.

While she waited, she dipped her fingers in the cool water, took a refreshing drink. She watched a large goanna go to quaff his fill. He took no notice of her. Neither, a few minutes later, did a brown snake. Live and let live, Zenith smiled, now watching some gadflies weave lacy patterns above the sun-dappled waters. She heard a soft explosion of children's laughter, and presently a piece of bark sailed by her. But she did not see any child.

When Steve came at last, he took a drink, too. Then he sat beside Zenith and dipped his fingers in the water as well.

'They've noticed the rise,' he told her.

'That's helpful. Anything else?'

'I could only speak with the old men.'

'You mean the younger ones still are away?'

'Yes, still hunting Avua.'

'The brave who broke the wailing and mourning rule and ran away?'

'Yes.'

Zenith dabbled for a few moments.

'I wonder why Avua did it,' she mused, 'he would know what would happen.'

'Why do men ever do things like that, knowing what can happen? The answer is easy. A woman, of course.'

'Why "of course"?'

'Because only a woman has that debil-debil power,' Steve replied.

'You're fabricating again!' she accused.

'Oh no, Miss Smith, it started with Eve and it's been going on ever since. If you still don't believe me I'll be more factual. Avua crept away from the wailing for only one reason. The reason's name is Ludy.'

'You said all this before,' she reminded him.

'I'm saying it again, but positively now. Ludy is in the camp, closely guarded, as she should be, upsetting a tradition like that.'

'She did nothing.'

'Only fluttered her eyes,' Steve said.

'Have they managed to meet?' asked Zenith.

'The young lovers? Oh, no. The guarding women have seen to that.'

'Then why have the younger men gone out looking for Avua? They should know he would head for here, not run off.'

'But head from what direction, from how far off? You have no idea how long a distance a fit young male

myall can cover in a few hours, and Avua, I've
gathered, is very young, very fit, very male. That's why
they're looking *away* from the camp for him, they know
he'll run for it but then double back. And there lies our
problem, Zenith. They way I've figured our approaching inundation, the hunters ... and the hunted ...
could be caught by the waters on the *other* side of the
tribe. They could be there for weeks, for months.'

'Leaving the old men and the women and children
unprotected?'

'Exactly. Now you've got it. We *must* get them into
Savage. Without the help and guidance of the younger
men they're pitifully vulnerable.' A pause. 'How's that
mime?'

'Mime?' she echoed.

'Well, you can't speak the language, can you?'

No, thought Zenith, she couldn't, but how to find
anyone to try mime on in this silent secret place? She
knew there were eyes watching them, she felt their
gaze, but where were those eyes?

Steve soon fixed that. He found the old men again,
leaving Zenith well in the background, for to have
brought her with him would have been a grave affront.

After some exchange, he bowed to the old men and
returned to Zenith.

'You're accepted,' he grinned.

'What magic did you use?'

'None. I simply said you were my woman, so had
come, too, to help.'

'Knowing I'm not?'

'Not what?'

'Your woman.' It was on the tip of Zenith's tongue to
add: 'But you, Mr Forbuck, are someone's man. You

are Helen's.' Ever since that morning at the bottom of
the steps when Derek Smith had brought Steve forward to address the meeting and Zenith had seen
Helen's alerted face, she had noticed a lot of other
things in Dad's secretary. A softness in Helen whenever Steve came near. A sharp consciousness of his
presence. A seemingly irresistible desire to brush past
him ... touch something of Steve's. Once she even had
seen Helen fingering a coat he had left hanging over a
chair.

'We'll argue whose woman later,' Steve said in answer. 'Immediately the old men will meet you, let you
see the women. After that you're on your own.'

'At least you could help.'

'Taboo,' Steve replied.

Zenith met the old men. They nodded gravely to her
bow, then conducted her beneath some bent-over river
gums to a camp by a branch of the stream. There were
not many women, for it was not a large tribe, but eight
adults and twelve piccaninnies were quite enough on
her plate, Zenith thought.

She began by cradling her arms and rocking back-
wards and forwards, saying the only aboriginal word
she knew for baby, probably not used by these myalls,
but they still might understand.

'*Birrahlee,*' she kept repeating. '*Birrahlee?*'

'Yes, they followed her, and several went into their
gunyahs and came out with infants.

So far so good, Zenith thought. She made the obvious gestures for an expectant mother. Any? she
asked.

They did not reply to that, but some of them glanced
to where the guarding women were standing. None of
these looked pregnant, so Zenith supposed they were

meaning Ludy, who Steve had said was expecting a baby. She decided wisely not to follow that up ... not yet.

Instead Zenith used all her school drama lessons to indicate danger, rising water, flood. She showed the gathering by taking them to the creek with her how already the water had come up, and they nodded back and looked apprehensive.

Zenith drove home the special perils for a *birrahlee*, for a piccaninny. She would have liked to have included a mother-to-be, but felt she had gone far enough for a first encounter.

Steve thought so, too, when later she joined him.

'You've given them something to talk about, to get frightened over.'

'I didn't want to scare them.'

'You've sown the seed, and you've done well. They'll chatter all night, anticipate all kind of debil-debils. Good for you, Zenith, making haste slowly may be a wise thing, but we haven't the time any more. Did you see Ludy?'

'Taboo,' Zenith sighed.

The Savage evacuation went on the next day. It would go on throughout the week. Although there was now a supplementary plane, the number that could be taken in both these minor craft from this minor strip was still meagre.

Derek Smith said over the next canteen meal ... all the meals were in the canteen now ... that it was going to be a slow process.

'Oh, for a jumbo jet!' he wished.

'When,' asked Carol, then she altered: 'I mean *if* the waters come——'

'When, dear,' corrected Derek gently.

'When the waters come and submerge the strip,' continued Carol, 'what happens then? I mean, if anyone is left?'

'There'll be someone left,' Derek answered her. 'Then, Carol, it will become a 'copter job.'

Carol pushed aside her plate, pushed it nervously, but she said nothing. Derek, not noticing her distaste, went on.

'But there'll be no need for anyone left here to avail themselves of any 'copter rescue because of any fear for their safety. As I said before, if the waters reached this highest spot after filling the cuts, then it would be curtains for everywhere, I should say. What do you think, Steve?'

'Goodbye, cruel world,' nodded Steve. 'Have no fears, Carol, you won't drown ... unless it's in your tears, for they will certainly flow. You've no idea of what it's like to be inundated, have you? I have. I don't mind admitting I've sat down and howled.

'You see, it's plain damn uncomfortable. There's wet everywhere. All privacy goes. You eat en masse, quite often using only your fingers, sometimes from a not too clean floor. When it really gets bad you wash en masse in secondhand water. Often you stay dirty. You can't launder your clothes, for there's nowhere to hang them, so you stay in them morning and night.

'Desert vegetation floats in, rots, and smells vile. Bush things come for shelter, things like rats, mice, the occasional snake. There are cockroaches.'

'Stop!' said Carol chokily. She left the canteen to stand at the door and stare out. Presently she went out.

'You were really quite cruel with her,' chided Helen ... Dad, noted Zenith, did not seem to have heard.

'Well, someone has to act mother,' Steve answered, and he looked suddenly at Helen, almost as if something had struck him in a flash.

Across the table the two of them stared directly at each other, the older woman, the younger man. They appeared to see no one else but themselves. It was only for a short time, Zenith supposed, but it seemed to go on and on.

Spring and autumn ... May and December. If it was good enough for an older man and a younger woman, for Dad and for Carol, wasn't it good enough for a younger man and an older woman? For Steve and Helen?

Pushing her own plate aside, Zenith left the canteen as well.

CHAPTER NINE

ZENITH did not go after Carol. Instead she walked down to the Cut, that first biggest hole of all around which Savage had unfortunately spread itself, never anticipating how large a working business it was eventually to become.

In those early days it had been the only cut, hence its name the Cut. The town encircling it now was unwisely placed, and had all this never happened, this approaching trial by water, Derek Smith had intended shifting Savage village to some more suitable location.

As she sauntered along Zenith realised wryly that, like the last time she had strolled this way, she wore no protective helmet. Well, no need for any helmet now, for all activity had stopped. No longer did the changeover whistle shrill, for there was no changeover, no outfits, no teams, no gangs, no workers.

She went to the viewing platform and stared down. The yellow ants scuttling across the base, crawling up the sides of the gaping hole, were there no more.

She tried to imagine the big hole filled with water, but found it impossible. Indeed she could not imagine any of Savage, her dry, cracked, red Savage, under water, yet what had Steve Forbuck said? ... 'It will simply creep in, spread, and you'll soon be wondering what it was like when it wasn't there.'

'What are you planning?' Steve had come up silently behind Zenith to join her on the viewing platform. 'Waterlilies? Some aquatic plants? A few coloured canoes to lend a festive touch?'

'Don't be silly!'

He contradicted, 'I think a little foolishness might be a good thing. God knows we have enough serious matters.'

'How serious? Dad has been at great pains to emphasise that there'll be no physical danger.'

'He's right. As he said, if the waters reached a height dangerous to this level, it wouldn't be just us up here, it would be everyone everywhere.'

'As you said: "Goodbye, cruel world."'

'Exactly. No, our serious matters are the obvious ones. Cessation of work for an unknown period . . . even possible cessation ad infinitum.'

'Ad infinitum . . . for ever?'

'Yes, my lady.'

'But—but ore doesn't disappear,' she protested. 'It's still there, it doesn't dissolve.'

'And how do you get at it from under the water?'

'But the water will seep away. Water does.'

'Yes, and I think it will, though I wouldn't care to hazard a guess as to how long the process will take.— On the other hand——'

'Yes?'

'The water, too, if it fills these cuts that your father has made—*could stay there*. It's happened before. You yourself must have seen inundated quarries that have stayed that way.'

'No, I haven't.'

'Then I have. Our home was not far away from a quarry—a fool place to put a home.'

'Then why did your parents——'

Steve Forbuck turned his gaze from the hole to look at Zenith.

'My *parents*?'

He said no more.

A minute went by in silence, then Zenith broke the quiet.

'Explain about the holes that don't drain off.'

Steve did.

'Some holes, most holes, drain. But some don't. You see, after you've finished with shale in Mother Earth you reach clay, and most clay is impervious.'

'Have we reached impervious clay in the Cut?' she asked.

'Not that we know of, but that's to be found out, isn't it?'

'What do *you* think?' she persisted.

'I just don't know ... but my bet would be that any water will drain off *in time*. So instead of Miss No Moneybags, Zenith, you'll still be the iron ore heiress. The trouble is you may have to wait, eventually sign over your promised coffers to your children, even your grandchildren, reap no benefit yourself.'

'That will be enough,' said Zenith stiffly. Presently she asked curiously : 'How do you know all this? About quarries, I mean.'

'I told you, our front door faced one. A fool position, as I said, and yet not one of the inmates met disaster there.'

'Inmates?' she queried.

'It was an orphanage,' he tossed.

She wanted to say: 'I'm sorry,' but forbore. Steve Forbuck was not the kind of man one apologised to, not in matters like that.

He did not notice any omission. He was staring out at the gap but evidently seeing another gap.

'I loved that old brick quarry. It was tumbledown, disused and overgrown. Age had made it quite attractive. Vines trailed over it. Gauzy insects flew across it. Water hyacinth had got into it—a curse, as I know now, but as I recall then very pretty. I think I got a little obsessed with the place, I know I got into a lot of trouble getting caught out of bounds there. Anyway, when I matriculated water and anything to do with it became my goal.'

'Hydrology.'

'You got it right,' he said sarcastically.

As if by mutual agreement they turned and wandered back to the town. Here they parted. Steve went to his bachelor digs, Zenith went down to the boss's house, for they were still sleeping there. She skipped supper, and went early to bed. She felt tired. It had been a long, hard day; all the days lately were long and hard.

She woke some time later to the sound of steps. It would be Dad and Carol coming back from the canteen. But it was not. If it had been that pair they would have come inside, done any talking they had to do in the comfort of the house. The talking now was being done outside the door, and in very low, inaudible voices. Zenith could not hear who spoke or what was said. Presently she heard the door close, and someone ... to go by the light steps, Carol ... come in, then go in her room.

She heard the other steps retreat from the house.

The next morning the final children were sent off, the last of the mothers and wives. On the female side now there only remained Helen, Carol and Zenith.

Tomorrow, Derek Smith said, the remaining men would begin to be listed.

'A lot of them are objecting, insisting they want to stay with the ship,' appreciated Derek, 'but I've told them it's no go. Steve predicts a closer settlement for all of us quite shortly, so we can't afford the space.'

'Yet you're allowing three women, Dad.' Zenith smiled at him.

'One of them, my daughter, is a disobedient baggage, so what hope have I of controlling her?'

'Carol?'

'Oh, yes, Carol.'

'. . . Helen.'

'Certainly Helen. Helen can't leave. Can't do without Helen.'

. . . Can't you, Dad? Can't you? Then do something about it. Pay Carol off—I may be wrong, but I'm still sure that Carol's the able-to-be-paid-off type, and then —then——

Then ask Helen, Zenith's thoughts raced on . . . only to stop at that.

Ask Helen what? she thought bleakly. How could Dad ask Helen when Helen's eyes followed someone else, lingered there? Why? Why do you do it, Helen? Why? *Why?*

Category Manual left, Category Clerical, then the exodus of the analyst, the liaison man, the bio-chemist, the other individual officers followed. Jake, the cook, was last.

Jake drew Zenith aside before he went and showed her all the stores he had collected for them. Each time a craft had flown in, on Jake's orders it had not flown in empty, it had brought in enough groceries to feed them for at least six months.

'Then after that,' said Jake, 'a helicopter can drop you a can or so. Well, good luck, Zennie. Keep your ammunition dry and you'll come through.'

'Dry when we're surrounded by water!' But Zenith was glad that Jake had said that. *Drinking* water! Had anyone attended to water to drink, not just to look at from the top of steps? Yes, Steve Forbuck had. There was an ample supply, he assured them. If that diminished they could always boil and purify the surrounding sea.

'So all's well in love and war,' he acclaimed.

'The war against encroaching waters, I accept,' dared Zenith, 'but where does the love come in?'

'Surely you can answer that,' he returned.

Oh, yes, I can answer it, Zenith said to herself, but can *you*? Yet she knew now that Steve in his turn was just as interested in Helen as Helen was in him; often she had seen Steve returning Helen's long looks with long looks of his own. But more bemused looks than the—well, tender look in Helen's eyes, more searching looks. Searching for what?

Zenith went out with Jake to the little airstrip. His would be the last plane out for today, and possibly for weeks.

'Ridiculous!' Carol had exploded when Steve Forbuck had warned this. 'There's still no flood signs anywhere.'

'Perhaps, but we have transport troubles,' Steve had

shrugged. 'The Heron we borrowed has been recalled by someone who evidently considers our worries are over, and our own Cessna badly needs an overhaul. You'd better consider that, Miss Quinn.'

'Consider what?'

'Consider whatever undecided young ladies do consider to help them make up their mind.'

Carol had not answered him.

There was a full load for this final exodus, the tiny waiting hut was crammed, and several passengers stood beside the white, upturned plastic buckets which comprised the best method of marking a bush strip.

Jake found a corner and began coaching Zenith on how to cook when you haven't anything to cook with. When the call came his last word was on eggs. He had left plenty of eggs, and some were sure to go bad. You tested them like this——

'Yes, yes. Good luck. A good project.' Zenith surprised Jake by reaching up and kissing him, then she stood and waved.

When she turned back at last she saw that Steve and Dad, who had come out as well in the small bus, had already left again in the bus. Self-absorbed pigs, they had not looked round for any other returning passenger. Now she would have to walk.

But, turning the corner of the shelter, one of the company jeeps still remained, so someone still was here. It was a hot, dry trek into town, and Zenith went forward eagerly ... then stopped.

Voices were floating out from the hut.

'I don't know what to do. I'm at the end of my tether trying to work out the best solution. I can't sleep at night trying to make up my mind. I'm actually quite ill reaching a decision.' It was Carol, shrill, disturbed.

'I'm the same ... only, of course, it's different for me.' It was Brent.

'Very different, you only stand to lose a job.'

'Yes, but a good one, for Savage is certainly that.'

'But I stand to lose ... well, what do I stand to lose? That's the torment of it, Brent, I simply don't know, do I?'

'You mean——'

'You know what I mean. How long will this wretched inundation go on? What will be the end result?'

'Ore can't disappear,' reassured Brent.

'But it can become unattainable.'

'True, Carol. Also the thing could take years.'

'I can't afford years,' she snapped.

'You are referring to——'

'You know what I'm referring to.'

'I believe I do, but in all fairness to me I think you should say it.'

'Then I am referring to what I would gain, or lose, *now* as Smith's wife. Not later but now. When this thing started, everything seemed rosy, the man was obviously a near-millionaire. But this has happened, or Forbuck says it will happen, and——'

'It is happening,' broke in Brent, 'I've gone into it with Steve Forbuck—I don't like him, but I'm convinced he knows what he's talking about—and it will happen all right.'

'Putting me?'

'You mean as Smith's wife?'

'Well, how otherwise could I participate?' Carol snorted.

'Then putting you in a very good position ... on

paper. The main legatee of a number of rich ore cuts, no less.'

'But actually? Not on paper?'

'Well, nothing at once. Nothing possibly for quite a while.'

'How long a while?' she demanded.

'None of us know. Perhaps if you had a family then your children——'

'I have no intention of providing Smith with children to inherit the riches I couldn't have,' said Carol sharply.

'Good, then,' said Brent in a completely changed voice, an *aware* voice, 'now we understand each other.'

'Do we?'

'I think we will, Carol. Unless I'm mistaken you're the kind of person I understand perfectly, someone, for example, who knows where they are going.'

'But I don't know. That's the worry. Advise me, Brent.'

'Well, you can't marry Smith at once, can you? Not now. Anyway, I happened to be there in the canteen that night he refused you.' Brent's voice was dry. 'I admired the way you took it.'

'I took it like that knowing I could alter him and his decision if I tried,' Carol said indifferently. 'A woman always can.'

'But you still can't marry him now. You couldn't even if the boss was agreeable. A plane might bring in stores, but it wouldn't bring in an obliging padre.'

'You don't need marriage lines to tie someone up,' Carol retorted contemptuously. 'It's just this: Am I wasting my time here? Would I be better out?'

'You're forgetting that that was the last plane.'

'A 'copter could come.' There was no nervousness in Carol now.

A silence followed. It was a long one. Brent broke it.

'You're really asking me whether you should lay down your tools now, or not, but only the future, not I, can answer. Perhaps it would be wiser, perhaps not. Perhaps, too, you may not regret holding on for a while if only for the fact that you're now officially engaged, something, I rather think, you haven't achieved before.'

'You're brutally frank, Brent,' she said coldly.

'Yet I think you appreciate that.'

'Yes, I do, but why should you think it?'

'Because men like Smith don't grow on trees, even for stunning beauties like you, and you were certainly waiting for a Smith.'

'. . . Am I really beautiful?' A lift to Carol's voice.

'You know damn well you are.'

Another silence, this time broken by Carol.

'You're quite right, I am. Also I've done my share of hunting—but been singularly unsuccessful. No doubt my requirements were too hard to fill. Oh, there've been many offers—you know what I mean.'

'I know exactly what you mean.'

Another pause . . . then Carol again, slyly, and with hidden mirth.

'I think you, too, have had your eyes wide open. I think you've been considering the boss's daughter. I must have spoiled that scheme when I happened along.'

'You mean with your beauty?'

'As well as my taking away what she would otherwise have got.'

'Well—yes. But frankly it wasn't such a blow to me. Zenith is all right, but never my cup of tea. Also at no time did that wretched girl give me a serious thought.'

'If she had you could have been my son-in-law,' Carol laughed softly at him.

'I can think of better relationships than that.' There were steps forward, and Zenith had to imagine the rest.

Eventually Carol said:

'You don't waste time, do you?' She sounded breathless.

'You're just what my kind of man orders.'

'And what kind is that?'

'Want me to show you again?' Another advance of steps. 'No? Then reluctantly I agree—there's no time right now. But briefly, Carol, it's that something in you that matches something in me, a coolness, a hard-headedness if you like, that one has to have. Listen, Carol, we'll go along for a while, play it easy. Actually, my dear, a girl like you needs something more than what Smith can give you, she needs a brain to match hers. A calculation, you could call it. With both our shrewdness added together nothing could stop us. We may not start at the top, even halfway, but——'

'In other words you're telling me to keep up the pretence?'

'At present. If it doesn't bear fruit—well, an engagement is soon broken.'

'A marriage is, too, these days,' shrugged Carol. 'No longer is wedded bliss expected to be for ever. Look, Brent, we'd better get back if the legend is to continue.'

'Done,' said Brent, and again there was that significant silence.

'I said we should leave,' Carol giggled, and Zenith rounded the next corner of the hut just in time.

When she emerged the jeep was a blot of red dust in the distance.

Scarcely seeing where she went because of the angry tears stinging her eyes, Zenith began to walk. She had only gone halfway when the red blot appeared again. A minute later the jeep stopped in front of Zenith with a screech of brakes. Carol fairly leapt out and came and faced Zenith.

'You were out there,' she said, and she jerked her head in the direction of the strip.

'Yes. I missed the bus.'

'But didn't miss something else!'

'Carol, I have nothing to say,' said Zenith flatly.

'Only hear, it seems. Then hear this. When we got back to Savage I went looking for you, for it seems we have to make some arrangement now over getting the meals. I was told you'd gone out, like we had, to the strip, but unlike us had not come back. I didn't have to be told *why*, though, I guessed at once. You overheard something, then didn't have the stomach to step out and face us. Well, you're facing me now, Zenith, so say whatever you wish.'

'I have nothing to say,' Zenith blurted in a low voice.

'Then I have. I'm sorry you overheard, for me it's an unnecessary nuisance. But since it's been done, we'll go on from there. Everything that was said was true, so I'm not lying about it. I came out here to Savage to Derek with one idea in my mind.'

'Marriage with Dad?'

'Of course.' A pause. 'The idea could still be there.'

'Oh, no,' came in Zenith, finding words at last, 'not now I know.'

'You mean you'd tell him.'

'Yes.'

'I don't think you will, though, not after this.' Carol wetted her lips. 'As you also overheard today, I've had my fill of project work—projects, so they say, offer more opportunity matrimonially. Well, they didn't offer it, not the kind I was after, to me.

'Anyway, following Silverstream Hydro ... I met Steve Forbuck there ... I decided to give projects a short break, and I took on temporary reception work.' Another pause. '*Medical* reception work.' Carol looked slyly at Zenith. 'I met your father there.'

'Met Dad? But Dad wasn't ... he didn't go ... he isn't ...'

'What reason did your father give for his last visit to Sydney?'

'Business.'

'He went,' said Carol bluntly, 'to a heart specialist because he was worried about himself.'

'Oh, no!' gasped Zenith.

'Oh, yes. I'm aware that it's not the thing for a doctor's secretary to talk away from her desk, but Derek came to the surgery because he was having some disturbing attacks.'

'I never knew—he never told me. Oh, poor Dad! But' ... gladly ... 'everything was all right, quite obviously it was all right. Look at him now.'

'It was not all right. Doctor Namoi, for whom I worked, imposes a strict self-rule. He never *tells* a patient. Now are you following me, Zenith?'

'No.'

'Your father has a dangerous heart condition, but he doesn't know it. Typing his medical history as I did, *I* knew it. And now so do you as well. Evidently physical effort, for he's been working hard, has not had any bad effect on him, so his type of heart must only suffer what Doctor Namoi always named stress origin. Are you understanding now?'

'I—I think so. You mean if I told him——'

'Yes. I'm glad you said *if*. You're a smart girl.'

'But I still don't believe you. Dad never mentioned any doctor. He just said he met you. I even think he spoke of a party.'

'Some party!' Carol smiled.

'I'll still check,' Zenith determined.

'Let me drive you in to do so.' Carol got back into the jeep, then opened the passenger's door. As she started back she asked:

'Mind if I check *you*, too, see you don't blab it all out like the raw child you still are?'

When they got into Savage, Zenith went straight to the office, Carol behind her. Because she was in front she could not see the sweet contrite face Carol put on, contrite for Derek's benefit.

'Dad, Carol has just told me you two met at a doctor's surgery.'

'Quite true, Zennie. I never told you before that I went to see Bill Namoi in case it would worry you, then I never told you afterwards because there was nothing to tell. You see, I was all right. Nothing worse, indeed, than indigestion. I never found the nerve to tell Jake that. He's gone still thinking he's the best cook in the world. But Carol, my dear, why are you raising it all now?'

'I'm sorry, Derek, it just happened to slip out. Please, darling, forgive a silly girl.' Carol stepped forward and held up her lovely face.

Ten minutes ago she had held up her face to someone else, she had said things that had dismayed and disgusted Zenith, things that Zenith had known should be passed on, but how could she do that now?

Not physical effort, Doctor Namoi had said, but stress.

Carol, beautiful, golden-haired, blue-eyed Carol meant stress, or at least the truth about her would mean that.

Zenith went out quickly.

CHAPTER TEN

ZENITH had never thought ahead to the time when Savage would actually be empty; she had trained herself now to accept the cessation of changeover whistles, silence in place of throbbing machines, but she had never in her mind's eye looked down at a town with nobody in it. The following morning she looked out and did, and in spite of all her warnings she was stunned. Robbed of its yellow-helmeted men, its small clusters of wives and children, the bare bones of the town became more prominent. It looked raw, primitive, and where buildings had not yet intruded it could have been lunar country.

A message had been received from Civil Aviation, and Derek Smith passed it round to the five who had remained on with him. He did it with a grin. The message confirmed what Steve Forbuck had already said: the cancellation of the loan of the Heron aircraft. Since the strip had worsened considerably since yesterday, this was no great disaster, especially when the authority went on to promise emergency calls, when requested, by a helicopter. Finally the message reminded Mr Smith that, since he had elected to go through with all this, it was presumed he would understand.

'Understand what?' demanded Zenith.

'That if you make your bed you lie on it,' her father said with another grin.

'Yes,' came in Steve Forbuck, 'but which bed? I've been studying the water position, and I want you, sir' ... to Derek Smith ... 'and the ladies' ... a glance at Carol and Zenith ... 'out of the boss's house tonight and up here on the summit.'

'Sleeping where?' demanded Carol.

'In the former bachelor barracks.'

'It's one big room,' she protested.

'Which can be made into two dormitories. Haven't you ever heard of the walls of Jericho and how they tumbled?' Steve winked.

'I've never slept in a dormitory in my life,' Carol objected, 'I've always had my own suite. Or' ... a placating smile at Derek ... 'a room.'

'Tonight it will be different,' shrugged Steve. Intentionally, Zenith felt, he was not addressing himself to *her*. He must have been aware, he couldn't help but be aware, of the protest, too, in the other lady he proposed to move, Zenith even felt it must show. She had absolutely no intention of sleeping next to Carol, sleeping in an empty office perhaps, even a corridor, but not in a dormitory with that person. Anyway, Steve was in too much of a hurry to move, or speak of moving, them. The boss's house still stood high and dry.

Helen as usual came in with a cheerful compromise.

'We've stacks of rugs, Miss Quinn. I'm sure we can work out something, make those walls of Jericho very concealing and very stout. Also I'm confident we can give everyone some private space.'

'But not until it's necessary,' grunted Zenith to herself, 'and in my opinion it's still not necessary.'

She made no audible comment, though, she made herself appear to accept Steve's ruling. She suggested sweetly to Helen that they start checking the stores, placing what they would need every day in a handy position, putting the less essential goods in a less prominent place.

'And when you're finished with that, pack what you'll need from the house,' Steve Forbuck called. He added: 'I mean it.'

So the pig had read her again!

Carol made a token appearance only in the store-room, then she disappeared. Zenith wondered how the girl would fill in her time, if one kept busy one had no opportunity to be bored, yet the possibility of Carol being bored did not trouble Zenith unduly. She and Helen had all they could handle, and more. Six people meant eighteen meals a day to be provided, for whatever else happened they all must be as fit and ready as possible.—Why six, though? Zenith thought resentfully. Dad had to be here, of course. She supposed Steve Forbuck had to. Then Dad himself had insisted on Helen. As the daughter of the concern, Zenith considered herself entitled. But why those others? Carol, she now knew bitterly, was still 'thinking', but surely Savage no longer needed an accountant, a Category Manual certainly, for muscle boys were always an asset, but never a 'Rithmetic Man like Brent was. However, Brent Davids had stayed on, and he had to be fed, too. Zenith put down a bag of sugar so forcefully it opened up and spilled out.

'Sorry, Helen,' she apologised.

'I think,' forgave Helen in her usual way, 'we're all on edge.'

'Not you. You never are. Particularly now.'

'Now?' Helen lifted her hazelnut eyes, those eyes that always reminded Zenith of somebody.

'I've watched you, Helen.' Tactfully Zenith did not say *when* she had watched. 'You're—well, I think lately you're—you're——'

'Yes?'

'It's mad, I know, but you're happier somehow, excited, elated.'

'Really, Zenith, that's mad!' smiled Helen.

'I suppose so. But you're not—well, sad, are you?'

'No, I'm not sad.'

'Is it because of Dad and what it appears might not happen after all? I mean, I see it like that.'

'What do you mean, Zenith?'

'Carol. Helen, it's all fading out, her and Dad, I mean. Can't you see that?'

'I haven't seen it, and any joy you think you see in me is not because of that.'

'Then you're not interested any more?'

'Interested?'

'In—Derek.'

'Zenith, change the subject.' Helen said it in that final way she used at times, and Zenith did—but only as far as to cut out Carol.

She returned to Derek Smith, returned nervously, her fingers fumbling the cans of groceries she was stacking.

'Helen——' she began.

'Yes, my dear?'

'Has Dad seemed in good health to you lately?'

'Never better. I was only thinking yesterday that crises suit him, stir up the adrenalin no doubt.'

'He's never complained to you?'

'Of his daughter, yes.'

'Not of his—not physically?'

'Definitely not. Physically he's on top of the world.'

... Or *looking* it, Zenith winced; heart cases some-times *look* on top.

The two women made up a roster for meal-getting. By silent agreement Carol was not included in the pro-gramme.

It fell to Zenith to provide today's meals, and she set to with an enthusiasm that surprised her. She really wanted to come through with flying colours. She might have, too, had not the stew she had prepared so faith-fully failed to cook in the time it should have.

'It's raw in places,' Zenith wept to Carol, who had come into the galley for something. She was so upset she did not care that it was to Carol she made the miserable announcement.

'It was boiling over when I last saw it, so I turned it down.'

'You might have told me! Now it's not ready, and dinner is in ten minutes.'

'Too bad. Tell them what happened, I don't mind.'

But Zenith didn't. How infantile she would sound crying out : 'This was going to be just right, but Carol spoiled it.'

'Like the curate's egg, good in parts,' said Steve later. He smiled maddeningly across at Zenith. 'Never mind, I'll ask the tribal chief this afternoon to allow one of the lubras to give you a cooking lesson.'

'No, thank you,' refused Zenith.

'Perhaps not, perhaps we'd better finish what we have on our plate first.—Sorry, Zenith.' Another maddening smile. 'Anyway, forget it, and instead get ready. We're due to see how things are out there.'

'Out where?' she asked.

'Out bush, of course.'

'*You* may be due, I'm not. I'm on meal duty.'

'More's the pity. But it doesn't take you all after-noon, or' ..., a look at the barely tasted stew ... 'it shouldn't.'

'I'm not coming,' she said firmly.

'But I'm depending on you to handle the women.'

'I think you're perfectly capable of handling them yourself.'

'Not one woman,' he fairly hissed at her.

'I'm about to clear up, Mr Forbuck, so will you clear out?'

'Gladly,' he said, and turned without another word and left. After he had gone Zenith was sorry. She had grown very interested in the camp, she really wanted to help, but through her own pigheadedness she had spoiled everything.

Recklessly she threw away the rest of the stew *and* the pan, for the change in temperatures had caused the concoction to stick. In centuries to come would some archaeologist unearth the pan and say to his students: 'Here we have an example of pre-inundation cooking.' More probably it would all be mummified, or whatever process happened under water, and no one would know what it was. But what was this inundation talk anyway? Zenith, looking out at the dry red earth under a dry blue sky, shook a disbelieving head. No water, no flood, she thought, and——

And no sleeping beside Carol for her. No, not to-night. Tonight Zenith Smith would rest in her own bed.

She did not announce it, though. When the last meal was over ... cold, and not too bad ... and when everyone had decided to settle, Zenith settled, too, until all the lights were out.

Brent had put up a row of rugs to divide the barracks into male and female sections, and Helen had done as well as she could to make the women sleepers private. But it still came down to Zenith sleeping beside Carol, so exactly twenty minutes after lights out, soft breathing each side of her, heavier breathing on the other side of the dividing rugs, occasionally a male snore, Zenith crept out.

The darkness beyond the barracks did not daunt her, she knew the descent to home like she knew the fingers on her hands. How often had she returned to the boss's house after a night at the canteen? Anyway, the desert was never dark, except for the hour after night fell until the first star pricked, all other times it was shining, luminous, dealing in big flowery stars, great gourds of moons. The interior made a lot of its nights.

Without any difficulty Zenith went home and slept in her own bed. How do you like that, Forbuck? was her last thought.

She did not know what wakened her. She lay still in her familiar bed for some minutes, then decided it must be that noise. Someone must have left a tap dripping and the impact made a soft wet slap.

She drifted again.

Then once more she opened her eyes. That last noise had been more ... well, splashy, if a noise could be that. She got out of bed, and her feet stood on damp floor. Damp!

She went out to the hallway and tried to see, but there were no stars and moon to help her here, so she stood in darkness. Also, as before, she stood on something wet. She moved forward. Still wet. Forward again, and this time wet up to her ankles.

Why—why, the whole place was damp!

There were matches in the kitchen, so Zenith padded out. She reached up to the dresser, got the box and ignited the match, then gasped. The kitchen floor was inches deep in water.

She found a lamp, lit it, and took the light to the back door. She did not gasp this time, she just stared in disbelief. As far as she could see, as far as the lamp could throw its light, was water. Because the house was set above the ground, two steps above it, and the water already had reached the floor of the house, she estimated the water outside would be well past her knees, in lower places much deeper.

It's come, Zenith thought.

The great snake has come up again and he has brought the river with him. That's what they would be saying out in the myall camp.

They would be bewildered, fearful, looking to each other for help ... looking for the man who had come out and told them all this before it happened, the woman who had asked about their babies. I *should* have gone, Zenith blamed herself, but then I never really believed any of this myself. Dad did, the rest of the project did, Steve Forbuck had every evidence to back him up, but in my heart I never really believed. Now ... her feet actually squelching, not just feeling damp ... I have to believe.

They'll be wondering about their men out in the camp, too, her tumbling thoughts ran on, their young

men probably caught on the other side of the inundation, unable to get home. They'll need their men.

Then there's Ludy, carrying Avua's baby, at least
we think it's Avua's baby, and there's Avua being
hunted but probably not caring, only wanting to get
back to his girl. Avua perhaps getting reckless about it,
and trying to cross and being—and being——

Zenith began to cry, a silly thing when already there
was too much wet.

One thing, it would do her no good staying here,
Zenith knew. She extinguished the light and went
down the hall to the front door. She would return and
with luck she might even be able to creep into the
barracks and no one ever know the foolish thing she
had done. She opened the door and stepped out ...
and the next moment was being swirled away in an
eddy.

It was not a strong eddy, and it petered out quite
soon, but it jerked Zenith into sharp awareness. What
was I saying about getting back unnoticed? she thought
wryly; I'll have to use all my wits to get back at all. No
longer was she thinking 'How do you like that, Forbuck?' for there was no one in the world that she would
sooner have seen descending on her than that pig-iron
of a man. He would know what to do, he always knew.
But he wasn't here, he was safely asleep with the others
at the top.

I've been an idiot. Zenith bit a trembling lip.

No other eddy had followed the first eddy. Zenith
decided it had come from that subterranean impulse
that Steve had demonstrated to her on the night of the
cooee trial, and like all such impulses it would have a
rhythmic pattern, so if she was to move she had better

move now, between the impulses. She ran down the path to the road that went up to the summit, trying to cheer herself with the assurance that once she started the ascent she should leave the water behind her.

By all dynamics she should have, but it soon became apparent to Zenith that dynamics were losing fast. Instead of leaving the water, with every upward step she seemed to be getting further into it. Probably she was in the current's path, and if she veered to the right or the left she might lose the force, but she remembered that the single track was strictly that, a narrow one-vehicle affair, and she did not fancy running into the unknown, for she had never left the thin, snaked road.

She put a foot forward, tested the ground, followed the foot by the other. She did this for about six steps, then an impulse caught her, and she was back where she had begun.

The next time it was harder going, the water seemed to be coming in a curve at her, driving her diagonally from the track she knew she must not leave. Again she forced one foot after the other, wishing she had something to hold on to when the measure of the impulse reached its peak, even a shrub would have helped, but here there were no shrubs.

Still she kept on.

She was breathing heavily now, putting all her strength into staying on her feet, advancing an inch or two. When the current eddied she lost those inches, but in the slack she caught up again, even won some distance, and if she could keep this up ...

But it was becoming apparent to Zenith that she could *not* keep it up, that fighting water needed someone much larger and stronger than she was.

It made it worse that she was within sight of the barracks now. So near and yet so far, she was crying; if I have to perish I would sooner perish out of sight of help.

At that moment she stumbled over a stone, and for a second she believed that her time for perishing had arrived. However, she righted herself, and as she did so an idea struck her. She might not be able to make the final distance herself, but at least she should be capable of hurling a stone and alerting someone.

Carefully she picked up the stone she had nearly destroyed herself on, mentally thanking her sports mistress at Retford who had decided that her talent lay in discus throwing, for at least the practice had given her direction and strength. She took a deep breath, then she hurled.

The stone certainly broke no window as she had hoped, for she would have heard that, but it must have done something, for at once she saw a light go on, then someone came to the door.

'Help,' she called hoarsely, 'help me, help me!' She lifted her arms to catch the beam from a torch that was now being flashed, then called: 'Help me, help me quickly, help me, please!'

She shouted it again and again.

CHAPTER ELEVEN

ZENITH was half-drowned by the time Steve Forbuck reached her. The water was not that deep, but every time there was an inward swirl, in her weakened state the long ripple knocked her over. She fell face forward into the flood impulse, forcing great volumes of muddy waste into her protesting lungs. When she emerged she gasped and choked for breath.

It was in the middle of a paroxysm that Steve caught her, then he carried her back to the top and up the steps. But he did not take her to the sleeping quarters, instead he opened up an office and there he lowered her into a chair.

He stood looking down at her for a moment, then left her, only to return almost at once with an armful of towels. He knelt down and began to unbutton her soaked pyjamas.

'No,' managed Zenith weakly.

'Yes,' he said firmly, and before she could try to protest again he was using those towels briskly, summoning up a circulation that fairly whipped through Zenith's blood.

When he had gone for the towels he must have grabbed up some fresh pyjamas, man size. He put them on her, buttoned them. They were absurdly large, but neither of them commented on that.

Now he was drying her hair, rubbing the towel up and down each soaked strand, testing the strand to see if it still was wet by holding it between his long fingers. When he was quite satisfied, he combed it, finishing by tying it back from her pale face with a length of office tape.

The last attention he bestowed on her was tea, tea laced with something more than just milk and sugar.

He waited until she had finished it, then said: 'Well?'

'I'm sorry.'

'You half-kill me, then have the temerity just to say "I'm sorry"!'

'Yes, I *am* sorry, Steve. But I half-killed only myself, not you, the water only reached over your knees.'

'You half-killed me *with worry*. When you called out, and when I saw you out there, I thought it was the end.'

'The end of a thorn in your side?'

'Yes, you could say that, but I still didn't want to see you die.'

'Thank you,' said Zenith wryly. 'You're waiting for an explanation, I can see that. Well, I have none. I just went down to sleep at the old house.'

'Out of sentiment?'

'. . . Yes.' It was an easy way out, Zenith thought.

'You little liar, you went because you wanted to defy me.'

'Well, I didn't believe you,' Zenith told him.

'You said you did.'

'I know, but I still didn't, not deep down.'

'You do now?'

'Oh, yes. Yet I still can't understand the *force* of the water. You gave us all to expect something that would just appear, something gradual. You said it would *creep* in, *spread*, they were your very words. And now this!' Zenith shivered.

'When water comes in anywhere it has to have some initial impulse, some primary impetus, and you happened to place yourself right there. The source here was that small leak I showed you once; it was at that spot that the subterranean system broke down and the swollen underground stream, swollen from the flood getaway from Big Billy, came to the top.'

'Not the big snake surfacing again and bringing the river with it.'

He actually permitted a grin, and shrugged.

'When the water leaves,' he went on, 'if you happen to be in the same spot down there you'll be flung off your feet again.'

'When,' she picked him up, 'not if, you said.'

'I still believe when. In which case' ... sourly ... 'you will promptly believe if. What is there about me, Zenith, that makes you like this?'

'Like what?'

'Opposite to everything I say or do, always on the defence.'

She did not answer him. Suddenly in that moment she knew that if she did she might have babbled: 'Because I *am* on the defence, defence for myself, for I don't want to be hurt, hurt in the way Dad is possibly going to be hurt by Carol, in the way people who love someone do get hurt ...' She halted her mental babbling sharply. The way people who do love someone do get hurt ... she had just said that to herself. But she didn't love ... she couldn't love ... Why, she disliked this man!

'You see,' she heard him say of her outward silence, and his voice in this wet world had a very dry note.

He withdrew from her, not only in person but actually. He crossed to the other side of the office and opened a window.

'Is that all?' Zenith asked.

'All?'

'To say to me? Aren't you going to—well——'

'Belt you? No, not today.'

She felt inexplicably angry, oddly deprived of something; it seemed an anti-climax after such a near-disaster.

'It's not today,' she muttered childishly, 'it's still night.'

'Correction, please, that was last night. Now it's today. Come and look.'

Zenith stood up, tightened the cord round the too generous waist of her pyjamas, and went and did so. It was still dark, but now more palely so. Even as she looked more lights appeared outside. She dropped her gaze from the fast-greying sky, lowered it to the earth, or where the earth should have been.

'Oh!' she gasped in disbelief.

The scene was so different from the Savage she knew that she felt that through the night she must have been secretly transported to some other place. A place of water as far as she could see, occasional higher levels where the ground vegetation showed up like cabbage tops, great patches barely water-covered yet, and fast, in the morning sun, turning to sticky mud. That sun seemed the most amazing part of it all to Zenith; if it

had been raining all this would have been understand-
able, but an inland sea, for it appeared that, under a
smiling blue sky she found almost beyond belief.

She turned and looked down the hill to the boss's
house, the house to which she had crept last night. The
water had sucked up to well past its windowsills.

'You see, you would have been drowned,' Steve
shrugged.

'But it can't be that deep everywhere.'

'No, only in the lower parts.'

'What about the Cut?'

'All the cuts would be affected, naturally. Holes
have to.'

'For—how long?'

'That's for time to tell us. Seen enough? Then hop
into your side of the walls of Jericho and get dressed.
Those male pyjamas could take some explaining away.'

'So could my female pyjamas drying in the office.'

He grinned and went back to get them.

Zenith tiptoed into the dormitory, found both
women still asleep, and dressed hurriedly.

She just made it before Helen opened her eyes, saw
the scene outside the window, then made amazed messages with her eyes at Zenith.

Zenith made agreeing messages back.

But Carol, when she woke, was very vocal. It
couldn't be ... it just couldn't be ...

'It is,' said Zenith factually. She waited, not a little
meanly, for Carol's next reaction.

Carol dressed quickly and went out to the canteen.
Helen had already produced tea and toast, and the
three men were at a table eating and conferring together.

Zenith, who had followed Carol, watched the girl as she stood at the door looking first at Derek, then at Brent. She never glanced at Steve. Carol seemed to be torn with indecision.

At that moment Brent looked up and caught Carol's eye. Zenith could see no message pass between them, all she could see was the merest flick of Brent's lashes. The next moment Carol was crossing to Derek Smith and bending over and kissing his forehead.

'Good morning, darling.'

'Good morning, my dear.' Derek sounded a little surprised ... but gratified. What man would not be gratified by such a pretty gesture from such a pretty girl so early in the morning?

'Here I was,' went on Derek, still bemused, 'wondering how I was to face you' ... he waved to what surrounded them outside ... 'and *you* face *me*, looking like a flower.'

'Thank you, Derek,' she smiled.

'No need to ask you if you slept last night ... something, incidentally, I also need not ask my daughter. Zenith, you look as though you've been through the mill.'

'It would have to be a water mill,' said Zenith wryly.

Before Derek could follow that up, Carol broke in : 'Oh, yes, the water. Water everywhere. How are the cuts faring, Derek?' She said it casually, but Zenith, looking down, saw that her pale pink nails were cutting into her palms.

'I can't tell you that yet, dear.'

'But you will, won't you? You'll let me be in it as soon as you know. What's vital to you, Derek, is vital to me, too.'

Carol leaned over and looked deeply into his eyes, and Zenith had a fair idea of what those eyes must be doing to Dad.

Gallantly Derek Smith reminded her: 'You are vital to me, Carol.'

Zenith could stand no more. She turned away.

After breakfast the three men went out to examine the cuts, or the cuts, anyway, that were able to be examined, for the inundation had not spread its waters fairly, and where some sections were well under flood, others only offered ankle-deep inconvenience, sometimes even less than that, just a sticky surface of mud.

When the men went, any pretence went from Carol. She looked out at the water with undisguised disgust and told Helen and Zenith just what she thought of Savage. No longer could Zenith retort: 'You know what to do' ... for Carol couldn't, not as she could have before. Any decision this time must be deliberate and final. It would entail a helicopter coming in to get her, and it would be a definite ... and significant ... step. No wonder the girl was hesitating like this.

But Carol ... temporarily ... lost any hesitancy at lunch, and it took quite a few flicks from Brent to steady her again.

Across the table Steve Forbuck looked at Zenith and said: 'I'm going out to the camp. I'll need you and I'm asking you to come. Will you?'

'Can we get there?' asked Zenith.

'That's for us to find out, but I think we can get some of the distance. I believe it will be all mud, but little worse than that yet. The important thing is can we get back.'

Up to then Carol had been paying no attention. She

knew, as they all knew, that there was a tribe somewhere out in the bush, and that Steve was interested in
them, but the conversation did not touch Carol until
Steve had tacked on to his 'The important thing is can
we get back' a succinct *With them.*

Carol put down her knife and fork with a clatter.

'With whom?'

'Four old men, some eight lubras and twelve piccaninnies. Am I right, Zenith?'

'Right,' Zenith said, putting down her knife and
fork, too, beginning to enjoy herself.

'Bring them where?'

'Here. Where else could they go?'

'You can't bring them here, there's nowhere, *nowhere.*'

'There's the verandah,' Zenith pointed out.

'They're people who have to live outside, they die if
they're not outside.'

'They'll die if they stay where they are. There is a
natural watercourse out there that grew into a stream,
but the stream had grown to a creek the last time we
saw it. By now it could be nearing an inland sea, for I
estimate that with the water currently feeding it sub-
terraneously it could reach—— Oh, hell, what's the
use of trying to tell *you?*'

'Steve,' Derek Smith came in quietly, authoritatively,
and Steve gnawed at his lip.

'Sorry,' he grunted.

Derek turned to Carol.

'These people will have to come in, my dear. Of
course they won't interfere with you, or any of us, in
any way. They will live, as Steve said, on the verandah,
and the little I know of them and their splendid in-

dependence I'm afraid it's going to be hard even to get them to do that.'

Carol's eyes were on her plate now. She was having a very difficult time. She did not want the party brought in, on the other hand until she found out what she was going to do——

Derek Smith closed the subject. He said gently: 'They will come in, Carol,' and Carol, swallowing, looked up and smiled weakly:

'As you say.'

It was not until Zenith and Steve were on the track to the camp, the jeep bogging, then recovering from its bog, every few minutes, that they permitted themselves the luxury of laughter. Steve even cut the engine to sit back and guffaw.

'When you said to her what's the use of trying to tell you I thought I'd expire,' gurgled Zenith.

'Your father soon put me in my place. Well, after all, she's his woman.'

'But she's not. She never was. Helen was that. Oh!' Zenith had bitten down on her tongue to stop herself.

'What's wrong?' Steve was starting the engine again.

... If you don't know, how can I tell you, Zenith fumed, you whom I've seen so often looking back at Helen when she looked at you?

She glanced sidewise at Steve in puzzlement. What sort of man was this who gazed tenderly ... yes, it had been tenderly ... at a woman, yet did not seem to mind when he was told she belonged to someone else?

'Seen enough?' He had taken his eyes briefly off the slushy track to challenge Zenith.

Zenith did not answer, and he looked again at the near-obliterated wheel prints between the root-submerged trees, and pushed deeper into the bush.

As they proceded it became apparent to both of them that the camp could no longer exist where it had existed before. The going became tougher with each turn of the wheel, and at one section the water almost reached up to their hub-caps.

'We'll have to give it up, do the rest on foot, that is if we can.' Steve gave a hunch. 'But first I'll turn the waggon, get her ready to move out again.' He chose a drier section, and after a long series of difficult manoeuvres managed to slew the jeep in the opposite direction, away from the camp site and headed back to Savage.

He came round and nodded to Zenith and she got out.

She went down in mud and water to the calves of her legs. It was not dangerous, but it made for very tiring walking. Neither of them wasted any effort in carrying on a conversation, they just trudged laboriously in the direction of the camp.

They seemed to go on for ever. Several times Zenith stopped herself from asking Steve if he had lost his way.

He must have sensed the question in her, though, for once he said. 'It seems longer because it's taking us longer. Every step here is equal to a dozen steps on dry terrain.'

'Where do you think they'll be?'

'Certainly not in the camp. Judging by the wet even at this juncture that would be completely impossible as it would now be well under water. No, I think we'll meet them presently walking away from it all, poor wretches.'

'And they'll have to keep walking, for we can't pack too many in the jeep.'

'No,' Steve agreed. He paused. 'Do *you* mind?' He flashed her an unexpected smile, and it lit up Zenith.

'Of course I don't mind,' she said warmly, 'the mothers with babies will need my space.'

'And a mother having a baby?'

'Certainly, if the bodyguard permits it.'

'I believe they will,' Steve said. 'I believe a lot of tribal lore will be confounded. The talks I had with the elders convinced me that they were very wise old men. I believe they had no two thoughts about breaking camp. I believe they even instructed the women.'

'No liberation, then?'

'Just continued female obedience,' he grinned.

'Is there any other direction they might have taken?' Zenith asked presently.

'Only this one. It's the sole *un*watery way, or less watery way, I should say, and they won't have any choice. Anyway, with all humility I do believe we've broken down any aversion they could have for us. I even think they'll be looking for us for help.'

At the next bend of the bush, Steve's words came true. In a miserable little crocodile the tribe came trudging towards them, the old men first, then the women, then the children walking behind. They did not run to their rescuers, they did not even smile or call out, but the oldest old man lifted his arm in a salute, and, like Steve's unexpected smile had just now, it lifted Zenith's heart.

They fitted as many into the waggon as they could without bogging it, then Steve revved up and his cargo started off.

Behind him, and almost as fast, for the track was near impossible now for a vehicle, came the others— and Zenith, Zenith holding the hand of a small naked piccaninny, then when the little uncomplaining mite fell into the mud a third time, taking the small boy in her arms and carrying him back.

When they reached the barracks, Helen and Derek were out to meet them, tactfully and gently to offer their comfort.

But Carol and Brent, Zenith noticed, stayed inside.

CHAPTER TWELVE

THE tribe were so quiet they might not have been there at all. As a race, they had that rare gift of silence, even in their soft-footed children. They moved like little winds that barely stir the petals of a flower. They had another quality of the wind: they were not seen. Actually they were seen, of course, they had to be, but it seemed to Zenith that she saw them seldom. Traditionally they had the power of disappearance; put a myall in a stand of trees and however scant the stand he was not there if he wished it that way.

But this was not the bush, it was an open verandah, yet still they seemed more absent than present. Even the little ones moved like shadows, spoke in wind-whisper voices. Are they here or not? Zenith sometimes asked herself.

The only problem with their food was the small amount they would accept. Steve said not to worry, that they would be supplementing it, but how could they do that on a little verandah surrounded with a sea of water?

'There are marshy bits, you know that yourself,' Steve pointed out, 'and in marsh you can find all kinds of goodies.'

'Goodies!' Carol, overhearing, shuddered. Although

the visitors never came into her life, never intruded, obviously she was hating every minute of their presence.

Zenith did not know how it was with Brent, whether he disliked it or abided it, for since that day at the airstrip, and the interchange she had overheard, she had had nothing to do with the accountant.

But Zenith did know one thing: all the myalls had much to do with Steve. Whenever he came on the scene their dark eyes followed him, whenever he communicated with them they hung on every gesture, every word.

'Quite the little god,' Brent said once.

'And not so little,' added Carol.

Not only the tribe but the rest of them turned to Steve Forbuck in the following week. Steve was the only one to go to for flood information. An amateur mark on a wall was of little use in an inundation of this proportion, since a level could be down one minute, then the next minute, stimulated by a sudden subterranean spasm, show high again. Only Steve, with his specialised learning, could give a reliable answer, and even he found it hard, so hard that Zenith, running into him one morning, recoiled for a moment.

'I thought you were some horrible monster from the deep!' she shivered, for he wore full diving gear from head to toe.

'Not from the deep but for the deep.' He looked down at his black outfit. 'Haven't you seen a wet suit before?'

'Not out here,' Zenith refused.

'For the reason there's never been wet out here. Now there is, so I'm going down.'

'D-down?' she queried.

'Well, I'm not going on a social call, not dressed like this.'

'Down where?' she asked.

'The Cut. It's the biggest, deepest and most important of the ore activity here, so should afford us the best information as to how things are going, how the bottoms are taking it all.'

'I wish you wouldn't,' Zenith said impulsively.

'Ignorance is bliss?' he interpreted. 'You're content to go on like this?'

'It's such a big dark hole,' she shivered.

'Don't tell me you're concerned about me!'

'Of course I'm concerned, I'd be concerned about anybody.'

'Thank you,' he shrugged. 'I'll find comfort in that in the murky depths.'

Although he told no one what he proposed to do, in the way things are found out in any camp it was soon discovered. When the Monster, as Zenith had called him, waded through the shallows round the summit to the edge of the Cut everyone was there, from the tribe who stood silent and apart to the group who stood silent, too, but as close to the edge of the Cut as they dared.

Zenith took a quick look at their faces, Dad's face very serious, Helen's crumpled with anxiety, Brent's unrevealing and Carol's face sharp and pinched. It's very important to Carol, she knew.

How *she* looked, she soon learned from the Monster.

'Cheer up,' he said, 'I'm coming back.'

About to make a deflating retort, Zenith turned away instead, her lip trembling. Then she felt his big hand on her shoulder.

'*I'm coming back, Zenith,*' Steve said again.

He did, of course, but it seemed ages before the surface of the water unfolded for him. In those minutes, for it was actually only minutes, Zenith went through the worst period in all her life. She pictured it down there, dark, obscure, threatening. How could anyone return from those frightening depths?

The watching tribe had come instinctively forward. If Steve had had some of their trust before, now he had all of it ... as well as awe. They might have been looking at a Dreamtime god, not a human diver, when Steve emerged.

Helen's cheeks were wet with tears of relief, and Derek was shaking Steve's hand. He and Helen hurried up to the canteen to make sure there was something hot and stiff for Steve when he came in.

The tribe went back. That left Brent, Carol and Zenith.

Brent looked at Carol ... looked promptingly? ... then Carol asked Steve:

'Did you find out?'

'Find out what?'

'You know ... the base.'

'Not conclusively in one go.'

'You mean you'll go again?' she gasped.

'Of course.'

'But you must have reached *some* conclusion.'

He said stiffly, 'I just told you not in one go.'

'But something? A hint? A pointer? An idea?'

'You're persistent, aren't you? All right then, I met clay down there.'

'Impervious clay?' It was Brent, and thickly, now.

'Clay is usually that,' shrugged Steve.

'Meaning?'

For an answer Steve only shrugged. 'Can I be spared, please,' he said plaintively, 'until I get out of this gear? It's not my idea of dressing for comfort.' He strode off, or at least he would have had he not been so weighed down.

The three followed in silence up to the canteen.

While Steve was being fortified, Zenith noticed that Brent and Carol were missing. She would have given much to be behind a curtain ... or the corner of a building ... to hear.

Whatever passed between them it was a different Carol who presented herself later. The sharpness and the pinch had gone, and Carol was all sweetness and light. She had even made an effort with the tribe. She smiled at the children, tried to entice them with some sugar lumps.

'You shouldn't do that, Carol,' Zenith began ... then saw that she need not have worried. The picca-ninnies were withdrawing from Carol, refusing her sugar bribes, hiding behind their mothers, the mothers were looking down to the floor.

Had it not been a complete surprise to Zenith she could have laughed over it all. Here was a perfectly lovely girl, a beauty under any circumstance, yet these people instinctively turned away from her.

'Why?' Zenith did not know she was muttering it aloud until Steve, who had paused, too, to watch the unsuccessful scene, drawled:

'That's what happens when you over-kill, when you try too hard. She did it to me; no doubt to every other man she decided might make the grade, *her* grade. And now where is she?'

'Engaged to be married to Dad,' Zenith said in a choked voice.

In spite of her poor reception, Carol kept up her sweetness. She kept smiling at the group on the verandah, smiling, Zenith thought once, until her facial muscles must ache.

She was nice to everybody, but most of all, naturally, to the boss. With Steve she was very careful. When he dived a second time, she did not question him, and if her eyes were trying to probe him, certainly Zenith anyhow saw no giveaway flicker.

Zenith even got to the stage of remonstrating with herself as to whether she had been unkind to Carol, if this was the real girl after all ... and then it all broke.

The crack in Carol's veneer came at noon that day, and not all Brent's looks could stop her from exploding.

'Good heavens,' she said sharply, 'that girl——!'

Zenith looked in the direction that Carol's eyes were looking and saw that 'that girl' was Ludy.

'Our mother-to-be?' she smiled.

'To be very soon, I should say. Oh, this is quite sickening! This is the utter end. As though it's not bad enough to be in a position like this, but to add to it all a maternity ward!'

Zenith had looked at Ludy again and decided that Ludy had indeed quickened. But why such a fuss from Carol, she thought? She wasn't giving birth.

She must have said so, for Carol turned on her, all pretence gone now. She was almost beyond words. But she did manage to say a few.

'This is going too far!' she threw at Zenith. 'Even in the possibility that the water will go reasonably soon, as Brent keeps reminding me, I can't, and I won't, wait any more. Big fish are only good catches so long as they remain big, and who knows what the end result will be? Whether it will be worth this ordeal or not? There is a limit, even to catch a millionaire. Meanwhile, while I wait, *if* I wait, I'm expected to accept this! *This!* Summed up, I think I'm beginning to agree with Brent when he says that two shrewd brains are better than one shrewd one ... mine ... and one soft one ... your father's. For Derek Smith must be soft, *he must be*, to allow a thing like this.'

'A thing like what, Carol?' Derek had come into the room.

Carol looked at him, suddenly at a loss for words, and Zenith took the opportunity to come in with: 'A thing like Ludy's approaching motherhood, Dad.'

'Oh, so you've noticed, too.'

'Noticed!' It was Carol once more.

Derek turned to his fiancée. Whether he had heard the previous exchange or not, whether he detected the note in her voice or not, Zenith did not know, nor could she tell by his prompt, quite pleasant: 'I'm glad you noticed then, because I've come to ask your help.'

'My—help?'

'All your help. You three women——'

'Three?' pounced Carol.

'I'm including Zenith, and Helen will naturally assist.'

'Naturally.' Again it was Carol.

'You three women,' continued Derek, 'all sisters with your darker sisters——'

'Sisters! That girl out there has her own sisters.'

'Exactly, Carol, but possibly inexperienced sisters, for you see, dear, Helen has been telling me that young Ludy's confinement could be a tricky one. First babies sometimes are, especially when the mother is little more than a child herself.'

Carol was backing away from Derek. 'You must be mad!' she exclaimed.

'But, dear——'

'This whole situation is mad! It was crazy right from the beginning. The only sane one in it has been Brent. Brent—are you there? Brent? Brent? *Brent*?'

Steve ran into Carol as she pushed through the doorway.

'He's in the communications room giving orders for things to be brought in by the 'copter,' he told Carol, 'also things' . . . a pause . . . 'to be taken out.'

He let Carol past and came into the room. 'What's this about Ludy?' he asked.

'Just a little case of motherhood,' said Derek quite smoothly, quite unruffled. 'Do you happen to have taken medicine as a sideline to water in your course at university? Specialised in the maternity side?'

'No.'

'Then keep out, Forbuck.'

'I'll help, Dad.' Zenith came forward.

'I'm depending on that, but depending most of all on Helen. It appears Helen did a year or so of nursing when she was young.'

'Did she?' Although he had been told to keep out, Steve came forward a few steps. His face was alight.

Derek did not see his expression, he was too busy organising.

'You two can keep up the hot water, keep the tribe pacified. After all, they're unused to our white ways. They could become suspicious.'

'Bring in some of their own women to help,' Zenith said.

'Yes, Helen advised that, too. Then you, Steve, you

have a pretty good rapport with them all, I think.'

'Leave it to me,' Steve assured him.

'And what about you, Dad?' Zenith asked slyly. 'You're doing a lot of supervising, but what about you in the actual work?'

'Not leaving me out, are you?' chuckled Derek, 'then I'll tell you what I'll be doing as well as supervising: I'll be helping Helen with the birth. Good heavens, girl, I had to help with yours. You chose to come along when Elvie and I were out at latitude ... oh, what does it matter now? Anyway, we were fossicking for—— There, I've forgotten that as well.'

'So long as you haven't forgotten the essentials, Father.'

'What I've forgotten Helen will remember.'

'Yes. Helen,' Steve said in a rather hoarse voice.

Zenith turned to look curiously at him, but whatever had touched him had left him now. Instead he was very alert. He took Zenith's arm and marched her to the galley.

'Water, water everywhere,' he said, 'but we need hot water.'

He put a match to the ring of their heating apparatus while Zenith began filling saucepans.

'I never knew Helen nursed once.' Zenith made the remark as she worked.

'I'd suspected it,' Steve said.

'How could you suspect it when I didn't?' At once Zenith flushed, and it was not from the heat of the now bubbling water. Of course Steve would know more, she told herself. They ... May and December ... had often talked together where two women had not.

Steve was unaware of Zenith's thoughts.

'I knew she'd done something before her secretarial work,' he said, 'she's often said as much.'

'*Distant* secretarial work.' Zenith was still resentful of his superior knowledge and she snapped it. 'Why distant, I wonder?'

'To get away from it all?' Steve asked.

'Get away from what?'

'Memories. Broken dreams. Oh, hell, how should I know?'

'You seem to know a lot of other things about her.'

'Not yet ... *not yet* ... but I do intend to,' he returned.

They worked in silence after that, Zenith a little sulkily, Steve abstractedly. She might as well have not been present, Zenith thought.

Finding a moment to spare, she crossed to the window to mull over it all ... then at once she withdrew again.

'Steve. *Steve!*' Zenith was speaking sharply now. 'Someone was looking in.'

'Who?'

'I don't know. A tribesman, but young, not old.'

'Where?' Steve crossed over to Zenith.

'There. A tall native. A young handsome native. We've only the old men in here.'

'We *had* only the old men,' Steve sighed. 'Stop here, Zenith, you may be needed. I'll find our friend, for the way we're situated he can't have got far.'

'How could he get here at all?' she wanted to know.

'Through the sticky shallows, not the deep watery bits, the same as the tribe did with us, though I have no doubt an inundation wouldn't worry him, these people can swim like fish.' Without another word Steve had gone.

He was away for quite a while. Derek Smith came down and directed his daughter to keep the water boiling. Everything was going all right, he reported from Helen. He did not notice that Steve was not there.

Zenith spent her time darting from boiling pots to misty windows for the next ten minutes, then Steve at last returned.

'It was Avua, Ludy's man,' he said laconically.

'Avua! How did he get here?'

'Walked or swam, I don't know, it was hard enough to find out what I did find out without demanding any embellishments.'

'I really meant how did he evade his pursuers?'

'*Has* he evaded them? That remains to be seen. But evading them enough to track Ludy to Savage must have been quite a feat, yet love lends wings, or so they say. The fact remains that Avua is here.' Steve sounded deeply disturbed.

'What's wrong?' Zenith asked.

'Everything, naturally. Naturally, too, I've sent him bush.'

'You've what?'

'Let me finish. I've sent him out there' ... Steve pointed ... 'until I get the feel of things here, know the lie of the land. You don't seem to understand the lore, Zenith, I don't, either, but I do understand more than you do. We're not dealing with town aboriginals, nor even mission ones, we're dealing with myalls, which means the original ones. In short the ones who are only up to what their grandparents' grandparents were up to, they're still not far from the Dreamtime. There's not many of them left, but there are some, and Avua belongs to them.'

'Belongs to yesterday, you mean? The big snake who took a river underground with him?'

'More than that, the importance of obeying old tribal rules. Perhaps most of all the mourning, wailing lore.' Steve sighed.

'The fact that a warrior was killed in that tribal skirmish a few weeks ago didn't matter over-much,' he went on, 'it was a reasonable killing, as I said once before all's fair in love and war. But the fact that Avua sneaked out when he should have spent the night lamenting, as has been done through the centuries, *did* matter. Avua not only displeased the enemy, *he offended and dismayed and outraged his tribe*, and that can't be forgiven.'

'Can't—or won't?'

'Isn't it the same in the end?'

'It needn't be if you—if you——'

'Oh, come off it, Zen, I might interfere with some things, but I would never dare interfere with that.'

'Then—then what happens?'

Steve only shrugged.

They stood looking at each other across the room in hopeless silence. Steve's eyes said 'I can't' ... Zenith's pleaded 'Try'.

A cry broke their hush, a cry unlike any other cry in the world. A baby's first new untried sound.

At the same time Zenith heard the whirr of an engine, a helicopter, but she heard it only vaguely, without reality. She was listening only to the cry, then saying:

'It's come! It's come, Steve!'

'Unto us a child is given,' said Steve in a low voice, and he crossed to Zenith and took her in his arms. He pressed her head to his shoulder, and Zenith left it there.

CHAPTER THIRTEEN

IT was Zenith who pulled away from the arms, those hard, muscular arms now almost incredibly gentle around her.

She went to the window and looked out, but even if a whole tribe of braves had stood outside and not just Avua she wouldn't have seen them. She was blind from brimming tears.

'Hi, what is this?' Steve had crossed after her, and his hand on Zenith's shoulder was no longer gentle. He forced her to look at him.

'Why the sudden aversion?' he demanded masterfully. 'I'm not the father, if that's causing your annoyance.'

'Don't be silly!' she said crossly.

'Don't *you* be silly,' he said back, 'one moment you're all over me——'

'I was not!'

'The next moment you're pushing me away. What is it, Zenith? *What is it?* And don't try to tell me that anything I've been sensing in you is imagination, because it isn't. I've seen you looking at me. I've watched you when you didn't know you were being watched. Unguarded moments ... *but true.* I'm sure they were true. There was that time at the Cut when I dived down and you went through agonies. Yes, you did, and it gave me a feeling I'd never known before.'

'Not even with—Helen?'

'Helen?' he echoed.

'There's something between you and Helen.' In spite of herself Zenith had to cry it out, had to release it. 'Steve, you can't deny it. You say you've watched me, then I have to tell you the same.'

'The same?' he questioned.

'About watching. I've watched you—and Helen.'

'Watched spring and autumn?' he said incredulously.

'You're nearer summer,' said Zenith cuttingly, 'anyway, I always said May and December. I tried to tell myself why not? After all, if it was good enough for Dad with Carol, why not with you with Helen? Why not a young man and an older woman as well as an older man and a young woman? Only——'

'Only you still didn't like it?'

'No, I didn't. I'd always wanted Helen for Dad.'

'But was that the only reason? No, Zenith, don't turn away, tell me. *Tell me.*'

'I have nothing to tell,' she said stubbornly.

'Haven't you? Haven't you?' Without another word his lips came down on hers.

For a while Zenith stood stiff and unresponsive. She could not, she would not concede to this man. Everything he was representing now was repugnant to her. Evidently the summer in him cried out for the spring in her, that was why he was holding her like this, but there was another shrewder side to him, the side that needed wisdom, maturity, something she had not.

'Zenith,' he was saying in her ear, 'don't hold out any

longer. You must have known even on that first day in the trading post when I manhandled you for the boy you were not that deep down this was beginning.'

'With other beginnings,' Zenith choked.

'I don't know what you're babbling about, and in this moment of birth, in this moment of the greatest joy man can know on earth, I have no intention of trying to find out. I have only intention for this.' Deliberately he drew her closer and kissed her again, but this was a different kiss. There was an aching hunger in it that Zenith could not have credited from this big, self-sufficient man, there was the authority and the command she had always known ... but there was something else as well. It was a thin tongue of fire that whipped through her veins, urging her on until she could suspend the moment of her response no longer. Without moving an inch nearer she was aware she had stepped *completely* across to him, recognizing the mission over, the conquest ended ... even though there was still—Helen.

'Helen,' she heard herself saying aloud.

'Yes, Helen.' Steve had let Zenith go, but only to arm's length. 'Zenith, I hope ... I think ... my God, I'm sure she's—my mother.'

'Your——' she faltered.

'My mother.'

'I don't understand,' whispered Zenith.

'I told you once I was an orphan,' he began.

'Yes, a home by a disused quarry, silver gnats, sun on green water.'

'It was a good home, a kind one. I had a good education. But like many of us——'

'Us?' she queried.

'The un-belonging ones, I still wanted to *know*.'

'About your parents?'

'Yes. I don't know if you know, for you've never been un-belonging, but there are places now to try.'

'Yes, I've read about them.'

'I went. It was no go, of course, it can't be unless the parents, or parent, try, too.'

'And Helen hadn't?'

'No.'

'Then?' she asked.

'But I was still told a few things, given a few pointers. My father was not living, in fact he had died before my birth. My mother had been very young, had had no family to turn to, no means, and in the end had done what they all had to do in those days, for there was no real, *tangible* help then, Zenith, or very little——'

'She had to give up her child?'

'Yes.'

'Poor Helen. But' ... frowning ... 'how do you know it was Helen?'

'The association I went to told me that after the birth the girl took on secretarial work, but always as far away from the cities as she could.'

'How would they know this? I thought there was a strict rule of secrecy.'

'There was, and there still is, for nothing could have persuaded the association to give me any names, not unless Helen, too, had come to them and asked.'

'Then how? *How*, Steve?'

'How did I find her, you mean? Despite the lack of information I still kept trying. I had only one reliable thing to go on, and it was the fact that my mother only took jobs *away* from towns. So I worked on that. As soon as I got my degree I started my search in earnest. You might have heard Carol say I had had projects before Savage.'

'You told me so yourself, you said you had a string.'

'Strings,' he said laconically, 'stretching over the years.'

'Looking for Helen?'

'Looking for my mother.'

'But you wouldn't have known her,' she pointed out.

'I knew that, I was aware that in only one chance in a million could a son, nearly thirty years afterwards, see himself, see himself *honestly*, not just what he wanted to see, in someone. Yet I still went on.'

'And you saw it in Helen? But you're not even alike. The setting of the eyes, I know that now, but not the colour, nothing.'

'No, I didn't see it, Zenith, but—I knew.'

'And Helen knew it, too.' Zenith was remembering that day that Savage had broken up and Dad had brought Steve Forbuck forward to address the crowd ... and how Helen had watched ... and watched ...

'I don't know—I think so. There's been nothing said, nothing. Oh, Zenith, I hope so. I even feel so. I feel there's something there we both are sharply aware of, I could stake my life on that. I don't care how it all came about, why she didn't keep me, I only know I want to keep her near me now. I want it badly, girl.'

'I want it badly for you, too, Steve, but more than that I want Helen—for Dad. But of course that can't be now.'

'Because of Carol?'

'Yes. I know my father, and he's one of the old breed, he'd never slip out of an agreement.'

'What if the other party slipped out instead?'

'Carol wouldn't,' she assured him.

'I may be wrong, but I don't think I am, and I believe Carol has already done that.'

'Slipped out——'

'Yes. You heard what she said in the common room before the birth began.'

'She was talking wildly.'

'Talking in a wild temper, you mean. She meant every word—I was convinced of that when I heard the 'copter. You must have heard it, too.'

'I always hear it bringing in the stores.'

'This chop was different, it was not the noise of a depositing operation, it was the noise of a taking away op.'

'Taking away?' she questioned.

'Taking away, Zenith. I believe when we go outside and see how the rest of the camp is doing, we'll find a camp smaller by two. By Carol and Brent.'

'Gone?'

'Gone, Zenith,' Steve said. He took her hand and they went as well.

It was curiously quiet outside, not the quiet demanded by a new baby, but a—a quiet quiet. Zenith said so to Steve in a hushed voice.

'Yes, it is,' he agreed. 'I wonder——'

'Yes, Steve?'

'I wonder if the tribe have left.'

'Left? But Ludy has just had her baby.'

'In their natural environs the women do that between their cooking, their gunyah cleaning, all their customary chores, so why should they change now?'

'I still don't like it,' worried Zenith. 'They may have

seen Avua, gone after him, the other young men might have arrived.'

'I think Derek can tell us that,' Steve said, and he called to Derek Smith standing with Helen at the end of the long corridor.

Derek and Helen came up the passage, and the first thing that Zenith noticed was that they came hand in -hand.

Her father saw his daughter looking ... how could he help noticing? Zenith's eyes were glued. He said gently: 'Do you mind, Zen? I know Elvie wouldn't have.'

'Elvie would have been glad.' Zenith kept her eyes from Helen ... from Steve's mother? ... she must wait, she told herself, for Helen to speak first.

But, immediately, where was the tribe?

'Left,' said Derek. 'The young mother with them.'

Helen broke in: 'And her son.'

'A miracle happened ... at least it seems that to me,' Derek said almost incredulously.

'The braves must have been hot on Avua's tracks,' he went on. 'Anyway, they arrived not long afterwards. Oh, yes, we knew Avua had come, the oldest old man indicated that even before Avua's arrival.'

'How would he know?' asked Zenith.

'How do any of them know?' said Derek. 'It's one of those things that belong to Australia's primal man. He just knew he'd come, and he knew, too, that the captors were closing in. So——'

'So?'

'So they all went out, and now, I think, they're one big camp again.'

'But Avua——'

'One camp *including* Avua, though I have no doubt
… would you have any doubt, Steve? … that several
severe restrictions have been put on that impetuous
young man.'

'No doubts at all,' Steve grinned.

'And the miracle?' Zenith reminded.

'*That* was the miracle. Acceptance of a son and
brother who had offended an ancient lore. And I think
I know why.' Derek looked at Steve again.

'You'd won their trust,' he said quietly. 'I said all
that before, but the day you put on a black suit and
went down into black waters you became something
more than a white man in whom they could put their
faith, you became——'

'But only the elders and the women saw it,' broke in
Zenith.

'The old wise men may not fight any more, but they
still win the battles. They still rule the tribe. Am I
right again, Steve?'

'Yes,' said Steve, 'there's not one young warrior who
would dare argue about that.'

'So Avua is forgiven?' Zenith asked.

'Not yet, but he will be.'

'So they're all a big family again?'

'Plus one.' It was Helen who smiled.

'So Carol left too soon, that is *if* she left——'

'She and Brent both left,' Derek confirmed, 'no
goodbye messages, no nothing, but communications
contacted us just now asking if we wanted *any more
personnel* taken out.'

'What did you say, Dad?'

'What do you think I would say? You tell her, Steve.'

'I think you said, sir, that a man doesn't leave a

goose that lays golden eggs to die in the desert.'

'There is no desert now, there's water,' pointed out Zenith.

'Water fast going down,' Steve corrected. 'I reported that to the boss the second day I dived. I also reported that the bottoms had only a small percentage of clay, insufficient to be impervious, that in two weeks, even less——'

'Yes?' asked Zenith.

'That you would be well on the way to be Miss Moneybags again.'

This time Zenith *did* look at Helen, dear, lovable, loved Helen, who was taking off her glasses, then putting them back.

'Miss Less than Moneybags?' she asked boldly. 'Now there's really to be a Mrs Moneybags.'

Everyone laughed.

But Zenith did not join in the laughter. Something was suddenly torturing her.

'Dad——' she blurted.

'Yes, Zennie?'

'That time you went down to Doctor Namoi——'

'And came back with the news about Carol?'

'Yes.'

'Look, can't we bury it, Zenith?'

'I—I thought ... Carol told me ... there was a possibility that ...'

'That you would be burying *me*?' Derek grinned.

'Well——'

'No, nothing of the sort, Zen,' Derek Smith went on. 'Bill Namoi only prescribed bicarb and a new cook.'

'But he does that, he never tells. That is, he only does on medical stories.'

'Which he didn't write. I'm telling you the truth, Zenith. He never even took up a pen.'

'But Carol said——'

'Then Carol lied. *Now* can we bury it, pet?' Derek turned to Steve and said plaintively: 'I've had enough of this soul-searching, Forbuck. Do you think, now that we might be functioning again in a week or so, we could search the cellar instead?'

'Done,' grinned Steve, and they went off.

For a long moment the two woman looked at each other, then Helen spoke.

'You're wondering how I could have done it, how I could have let my baby go?'

'No, no, of course not,' Zenith protested. Then she said: 'Yes.'

'I was young—as young as you are. I literally had nobody, Zenith. My parents had died, and, hoping to be able to turn a page, I came to a new state. I met Gareth ... young, too ... no family either ... and we married. He met with a fatal accident almost at once. He never saw the baby, he never even knew there was going to be a baby. It was that quick.'

'Oh, Helen!' sighed Zenith.

'It was different then, you have no idea how different. Unless you had a family to turn to, or friends, then you couldn't—you couldn't——'

'I understand, dear.'

'They told me how selfish I would be to attempt it, how unfair. I could see they were only trying to help me, so—I gave him up.'

'Was he Steve then?' Zenith asked.

'No, only a male child.' Helen choked a little. 'I remember that on the record I had to sign. Male child.'

'What about the Forbuck?'

'I believe they used to go through a long list of sur-names.' Helen half-choked again. 'Gareth's name was Saunders,' she said.

After a while she went on.

'Zenith, that's all I can remember. He was Gareth Saunders, and we were young, and we fell in love. It's thirty years ago now. Perhaps it would have been won-derful, perhaps with our immaturity it would not, I don't know, but I do know this, that it couldn't have been more wonderful than the feeling I have, and al-ways have had, for Derek.'

'Then,' said Zenith, 'that's all anyone could ask.'

The two women went down the corridor with their arms entwined, but halfway to the canteen Zenith stopped.

'It *is* falling, Helen,' she called excitedly, 'you can even see the front steps of the boss's house now.' She pointed down the slope.

Helen released herself from Zenith and went along the passage to tell Derek the glad news, and Steve For-buck, discreetly leaving the two of them together, came out to Zenith.

'A thought has just struck me,' he grinned, 'if I'm Helen's son, and I am, and I marry Helen's husband's daughter, which I will, I shall be marrying my sister. How do you like that?'

'As brother material, not at all,' Zenith admitted, 'but as a husband——'

He stepped intentionally forward. 'Yes?'

'No, not here, Steve, not with all the world watch-ing.'

'One hawk, one harrier, one—— Zenith, *Zenith*, did

you hear what I just said? They're back.' He pointed
far upward. 'The birds are back. The next it will be
the frogs again. In a week or so the Savages.'

'But not Alexander,' regretted Zenith. 'Alexander's
parents signed up for another project. Alexander won't
return.'

'So we'll have to get our own Alexander, won't we,
supply our own bundle of trouble. Quickly, darling,
when did you say the padre flies in?'

'Under these conditions he would only come on de-
mand. Steve, Steve, what are you doing?' For Steve
was pulling Zenith along with him down to the end
door.

'I'm contacting communications with an urgent
memo,' he told her, 'a message to be delivered *at once*.'

He took up a pen and wrote. Then he said: 'This is
it.

'To the Reverend William Flett, Inland Mission.
Please come at once Stop Subject Marriage Stop SOS
Signed Zenith and Steven Stop——'

'Oh, you idiot!' Zenith told him.

'But,' she added, 'you very special one.'

And there's still *more* love in

Harlequin Presents...

Yes!

Four more spellbinding
romantic stories every month
by your favorite authors.
Elegant and sophisticated tales of
love and love's conflicts.

Let your imagination be swept away to
exotic places in search of adventure,
intrigue and romance. Get to
know the warm, true-to-life
characters. Share the special
kind of miracle that
love can be.

Don't miss out. Buy now and discover
the world of HARLEQUIN PRESENTS...

Do you have a favorite Harlequin author? Then here is an opportunity you must not miss!

What the press says about Harlequin Romances...

"...clean, wholesome fiction...always with an upbeat, happy ending."
— *San Francisco Chronicle*

"...a work of art."
— *The Globe & Mail,* Toronto

"Nothing quite like it has happened since *Gone With the Wind...*"
— *Los Angeles Times*

"...among the top ten..."
— *International Herald-Tribune,* Paris

"The most popular reading matter of American women today."
— *The Detroit News*

"Women have come to trust these clean easy-to-read stories about contemporary people, set in exciting foreign places."
—*Best Sellers*, New York

"Harlequin novels have a vast and loyal readership."
— *Toronto Star*